"I'm not the kind of woman you're used to,"

Abby said.

"You have no idea what I'm used to," Houston replied with an edge to his voice. "Tell you what, Miss Abigail, let's say you and I agree not to deal in generalities. I'll refrain from making any misleading assumptions about you, and you do the same about me."

"Misleading? You think I've misled you?" Was it possible he knew who she was? Why she was here?

"I think you're a beautiful woman. And I think finding out who you are is going to be one sweet adventure."

"You may be disappointed."

"Why?"

"This is it. Plain and simple. No deep, dark secrets. No hidden agenda," she lied. "I'm just what I appear to be."

"No one," he said, "is just what they appear to be. And everyone has secrets. Some darker than others."

Dear Reader,

Wow! What a month we've got for you. Take *Maddy Lawrence's Big Adventure*, Linda Turner's newest. Like most of us, Maddy's lived a pretty calm life, maybe even too calm. But all that's about to change, because now Ace Mackenzie is on the job. Don't miss this wonderful book.

We've got some great miniseries this month, too. *The One Worth Waiting For* is the latest of Alicia Scott's THE GUINESS GANG, while Cathryn Clare continues ASSIGNMENT: ROMANCE with *The Honeymoon Assignment*. Plus Sandy Steen is back with the suspenseful—and sexy—*Hunting Houston*. Then there's Beverly Bird's *Undercover Cowboy*, which successfully mixes romance and danger for a powerhouse read. Finally, try Lee Karr's *Child of the Night* if you enjoy a book where things are never quite what they seem.

Then come back again next month, because you won't want to miss some of the best romantic reading around—only in Silhouette Intimate Moments.

Enjoy!

Leslie Wainger
Senior Editor and Editorial Coordinator

Please address questions and book requests to:
Silhouette Reader Service
U.S.: 3010 Walden Ave., P.O. Box 1325, Buffalo, NY 14269
Canadian: P.O. Box 609, Fort Erie, Ont. L2A 5X3

HUNTING HOUSTON

SANDY STEEN

Published by Silhouette Books

America's Publisher of Contemporary Romance

 SILHOUETTE BOOKS

ISBN 0-373-07710-6

HUNTING HOUSTON

SANDY STEEN

Hooked on romance since she read *Gone With The Wind* at age twelve, Sandy credits dedicated teachers who stressed the benefits of a solid reading foundation for a major part of her success. Since her first book was published, she has repeatedly made the Waldenbooks bestseller list, received a *Romantic Times* KISS Award and was nominated for the 1994 *Romantic Times* Reader's Choice Award.

A native Texan, Sandy leads a busy life as an author, mother of two and grandmother of one. But most of all, she is a lover of romance in print, on the screen and, of course, in real life.

For the Three Amigos.
May we live long and travel.

Prologue

A steady wind filled the sails, sending the sixty-four-foot catamaran, *Two of a Kind*, skimming over the ocean like a hawk on the wing. Headed south by southwest, toward the big island of Hawaii, her twin hulls rhythmically rose and fell with the waves, and off her port side the blazing orange-red sun dipped lower and lower into the Pacific.

At the helm, Houston Sinclair turned his face to the wind, savoring the soul-deep peace that always enveloped him when he was on the open sea. In the past half hour the wind had picked up considerably, and the swells were climbing. Houston didn't mind in the least. For him, the sea was always a challenge, always an adventure.

He took a deep breath, filling his lungs with sea air, feeling right with the world.

Then the world exploded beneath his feet.

One second he was standing on deck. The next, he was flying through the air.

He hit the water on his right side, almost in a fetal position. Instantly, the ocean closed over him like a shroud.

Stunned by the impact, he sank deeper and deeper. Bubbles, millions of them, filled with life-giving air, surrounded him. He was smothered in a whirlpool of bubbles, and for a terrifying second that felt like an agonizing eternity, he couldn't tell which way was up. Which way was the surface?

He panicked.

Kicking and groping wildly, he grappled with the bubbles, his mind screaming for sanity, his lungs screaming for air. Finally, the instinct for survival, darkly primordial and powerful, took control, forcing him to look up, to follow the bubbles. His lungs burning, he clawed his way toward air, toward life. Seconds later, his head broke the surface, his body shooting out of the water like a missile as he gasped for breath. Dazed and disoriented, he went under again, and shot back up, coughing, choking—and deliriously happy to suck in sweet, life-giving air. A wave picked him up, pausing for an instant, then dropped, crashing over him. This time he fought to stay afloat, and won.

In that brief, stunning moment Houston got a good look at the *Two of a Kind.*

Her right hull was damaged and partially submerged. The rest of her was almost completely engulfed in flames.

Another wave snatched him up, and from his watery perch, the sky, the water, the whole world looked aflame. The last rays of the sun blasted across the tumultuous horizon, turning the sky blood red, fed like a transfusion by the flames from the blazing ship. The churning water reflected the God-made and man-made infernos, forming a flaming trinity of destruction.

"Shelley!" he screamed, realization hitting him for the first time. He tried to swim for the boat but another wave hauled him up, then down, impeding his progress, carrying him farther away from the wounded catamaran. "Shelley! Shelley, where are you?"

She had gone below to make coffee a few moments before—

A few moments before the explosion.

Oh, God, no! Please, no!

The thought that his partner's beautiful, loving wife might be injured, or worse, made his blood run cold. He had to get to her.

Fighting the roller-coaster waves was futile. The harder he tried, the more distance the waves put between him and the boat. Houston knew the only way to reach it was underwater. He took a deep breath, preparing to dive, then stopped.

He couldn't do it.

For a half a heartbeat panic reared its ugly head, and the thought streaked through his mind that if he went under he might not come up. This time the sea would keep him.

Finally, the image of Shelley waiting for help, waiting for him, shoved panic aside, and he dove beneath the surface. With light from the flames to aid him, Houston swam hard until he was only a few yards from the catamaran. Underwater he could see that the right pontoon, the one connected to the tiny galley, wasn't just damaged.

It was shattered.

His head broke the surface. Flames ate away at the sleek-lined craft, crackling and popping like the laughter of demons.

"Shelley! Shelley, answer me!"

But there was no answer.

He had no idea what had caused the explosion, but the cause didn't matter so much as the thought that it might trigger another. If that happened . . .

He *had* to get to Shelley. Now!

The ship was taking on water. Flames leaped higher and higher over the remaining hull, cracking, hissing. The stench of burning fiberglass filled his nostrils while the wind and waves, in league to separate him from the boat, tried to drown him. In the low point between waves, he tried to swim at an angle, treading water and riding the ever-increasing swells, trying to make it to the starboard side.

Please, he prayed. Let her have been headed topside. And not in the galley!

Finally, by lunging through the water more than swimming, Houston managed to maneuver himself around the boat. Thankfully, a portion of the left hull and the wheelhouse were not on fire. But for how long? The fuel tanks were virtually full. The rest could go any minute. And the sun was almost gone.

He had to get to her.

"Shel—" A mouthful of water cut him off as a wave slammed him into the jagged opening of the damaged hull. Pain, quick and hot, shot down his leg. He screamed, the sound abbreviating to tortured gurgles as he slipped beneath the surface. He shot back up, fighting the waves. Fighting the pain.

Forget the pain. Forget everything but Shelley.

He had to get to her. The probability of another explosion increased with every passing second.

Determined to find her, Houston hauled himself on board the sinking ship, flopping onto the slanted, heaving deck.

"Shelley!" he called, trying to see through the billowing smoke.

"Hou-Houston," finally came a choked response accompanied by the *thunk-thunk* of a muted bell.

"Thank God!" The heat from the flames scorched his face and the smoke thickened. She had to be topside, he decided. Near the bow. Probably holding on to the ship's bell.

"I'm coming, Shel. Hang on!"

He started crawling to the starboard side, trying to make his way around the fire, make his way to her, then stopped.

The raft! He had to have the raft. *Can't survive without it.*

"Houston. Hurry, hurry," Shelley called again, her voice fading.

He turned his head toward the sound of her voice, weak, helpless, imploring, then turned to look at the section of molded fiberglass that served as both a bench seat and storage locker.

Then he glanced at his leg.

Bright red blood streamed down his calf from a nasty-looking gash, and mingled with seawater. With his leg cut—and no telling what injuries Shelley might have—they couldn't survive in the open sea. They would be shark bait before the first star was visible. They *had* to have the raft.

"Hang on, Shel. Just hang on."

As fast as he could, Houston crawled on his belly to the locker, yanked off the smoldering seat cushion, and reached for the two-man inflatable raft that was stored inside. With his body stretched across the deck, and his feet in the rising water, he flung the raft away from the flames and into the waves.

It inflated instantly.

Immediately, he rolled onto his belly and started crawling back up the deck. Knowing Shelley was trusting him to save her, he drove himself on, virtually ignoring what was fast becoming a wall of flames. Literally pulling himself hand over hand along the stainless-steel railing that edged the engine compartment and wheelhouse, he made his way toward the sound of her voice—a sound that grew weaker with every call.

He reached the end of the rail, his body now at almost a forty-five degree angle from the surface of the choppy water as the right hull sank deeper into the ocean, pushing the left hull into the air. Holding on with one hand, he extended his other arm as far as it would go, straining to grasp the wheel just out of reach. Finally, desperately, he lunged upward, grabbed for the wheel, and missed. His body slammed back against the deck, jarring loose his hold on the rail.

He slid back down into the churning sea.

Frantically, he tried to climb back on board, but wave after powerful wave mercilessly pulled at his body until it ripped his hands away. A massive swell jerked him up, and flung him yards from the fatally wounded catamaran.

"Houston!" Shelley screeched, her voice barely carrying over the sound of the fire and the waves crashing against the ship.

Frustrated, scared and bobbing amid the relentless swells like a cork, he waved his arms in the air, hoping she would see him. "Jump, Shelley! Just jump!"

If she saw him, he never knew.

If she heard him, called out to him, he never heard it.

The explosion drowned out sight, sound. Everything.

"Shelley-y-y!" Houston screamed, as tiny shards of debris rained down on him.

The blast lit up the ever-darkening sky, the force turning an unruly sea into a churning cauldron. Enormous waves pushed out in rings, shoving him even farther away. Far enough to see that the front of the remaining hull was gone.

Blown away.

The ship was sinking quickly now, with nothing of the catamaran left above the waterline save the top of the main mast.

He called Shelly's name over and over, telling himself that if he had been thrown clear by the first explosion, the same thing could have happened to her.

But there was no answer.

As Houston watched, the mast of the *Two of a Kind* shot straight up in the air riding the crest of a mammoth wave, then vanished. Gone, was all he could think. Still, he clung to the threadbare hope that somehow Shelley had survived the explosion. He had to find her.

The raft? He had to get to the raft, so he could find her.

Through water-blurred vision he scanned the surface, finally spotting the inflated raft with its glow-in-the-dark markings. It looked so far away that for a fleeting moment despair swamped him along with the next wave. He hung in the water for long moments, the light gone, surrounded by darkness above and below. His mind spiraled toward surrender, toward giving up.

Beneath the surface, something slithered past his leg.

Cold, bloodcurdling terror exploded through his body, and any second he expected to be yanked under.

Survive! instinct demanded.

And survival was the raft.

He swam toward the floating lifesaver, his strokes as fluid as he could make them. And with each stroke, each kick, he wondered if it would be his last. With each breath he expected to feel powerful jaws take him under.

What in fact was only minutes, passed like hours before he reached the raft that seemed to deliberately bob just out of his grasp. Finally, he grabbed the side, and hauled himself up and over into the raft. He looked around, expecting to see fins break the surface, but there was nothing. His heart racing like a runaway train, he took deep, calming breaths.

"Okay," he gasped, his saltwater-raspy voice, his harsh breathing sounding strange to his own ears. "Paddles." He unstrapped the two small plastic paddles, then looked over the vast expanse of water. Paddle where?

A streak of white atop a wave caught his attention. "I see it!" he yelled, as if he had just seen a rescue ship on the horizon.

Maybe it was a piece of the boat big enough for Shelley to hang on to. Houston paddled like a man in a race with the devil himself, finally reaching the "patch" of white.

It was a piece of the boat. A flat piece of fiberglass approximately two feet long, one foot wide.

And mounted to its surface was the ship's bell.

The clanger, no longer the clarion of nautical time, was twisted into a snarled ribbon of brass, and its bulb was gone. With each rise and fall of a wave, the misshapen clanger hit the side of the bell with a weak scratching sound, almost like a pitiful whimper.

Houston watched it bob in the water, heard its dead ring tolling the truth he couldn't face.

"No-o-o!"

His anguished cry was carried away like the last piece of the boat floating farther and farther away.

No! He had to try again. She was out there somewhere. She had to be.

So, he tried again. Searched again. And again. He had to find her. He had to!

He paddled until his arms felt as if they would fall off, circling what he thought was the immediate area where the boat had gone down. He called her name. Repeatedly. Incessantly.

He called until his voice gave out.

He paddled until the sun came up.

But there was nothing to see but miles and miles of empty Pacific.

At some point during the night, the winds had died, the waves calmed, almost as if, having claimed its sacrifice, the sea could again become the gentle rolling beauty that had seduced men since the beginning of time.

At some point during the night, Houston had known his efforts were futile, but he'd persisted. Not even the gash along his left shin and the second-degree burns on his arms and shoulder had stopped him. The pain from his injuries was nothing compared to the pain in his heart. The pain of facing the hideous truth.

He had made the wrong choice. And because of it, Shelley had died.

There had been a moment—maybe a half a moment—when he'd had to decide between going for Shelley first, or going for the raft. He'd chosen the raft. And while logic dictated he had made a sensible decision, shattered self-respect insisted otherwise. He had thought about his wound, about facing sharks, and in those few precious seconds he had lost any advantage he had in saving Shelley. To call what he had done an act of selfishness was pitifully inadequate.

He was a coward.

And he would die a coward.

His leg throbbed and his wound festered. Soon fever would take his sanity. It was only a matter of time before he died of infection or thirst. Or madness. Eyes closed, his face to the ever-brightening sun, he lay spent, mentally and physically.

And hopelessly adrift.

When he opened his eyes again, it was to a star-filled night sky. Waves gently rocked him in his inflated cradle. For a moment he didn't realize where he was, and gave himself over to the soothing motion. A part of his now feverish mind wanted to go on forever, rocking, drifting. He would just go back to sleep and drift forever.

He could drift up to the stars, then. To their twinkling light that looked so clean. So welcoming. If he could just reach out and touch them . . .

"'Star light, star bright,'" he whispered, trying to remember a piece of poetry from his childhood. "'First star I see . . .'" But there wasn't just one star. The sky was filled with them. Millions and millions.

"'Starry, starry night . . .'" he croaked, his overheated brain switching from poetry to the words to an old song. Pretty stars. Nice stars.

In his delirium he was certain that the shimmering constellations heard him. Certain they sparkled back in response. They were his friends. They were there to keep him company.

"'Paint your palette blue and gray . . .'" Pretty melody. Nice melody.

It joined the rhythm of the waves, and in tandem they rocked him, rocked him.

"'Look out on a summer's day,'" he rasped, trying to stay in tune. He looked up at the stars. It wasn't day. It was night. Dark. "Eyes that see dark . . . darkness in my soul."

No, he didn't want to think about that. Look at the stars. Hang on to the stars, he told himself.

Some minimally functioning, logical part of his fevered mind told him to forget about stars, and concentrate on survival; assured him that his partner, Gil, would start rescue proceedings as soon as he realized the ship was overdue. Gil would find him.

Gil.

The name echoed through Houston's barely conscious mind. His partner. Lifelong friend. Shelley's husband.

But Shelley was dead.

And it was his fault.

Memories shoved and pushed, jostled for position in his fever-fuzzy brain. No, no. He didn't want to remember. Remembering hurt too much. Much too much...

No. Better not to remember. Just think about the stars. Stars so pretty against the sky. Dark sky. Dark...dark...

Chapter 1

"How would you like to take a little trip to Hawaii?" Braxton Hall asked, plopping himself into the ancient wingback chair Abigail Douglass reserved for visitors.

"I've already had my vacation," Abby replied, remembering the week she had spent at a friend's isolated cabin in the mountains some ten months past. Solitary time. Time she had needed to rebalance herself.

"That was almost a year ago."

Abby shrugged, knowing full well he was about to hand her a new case, not airline tickets. "We redheads sunburn so easily." She lifted a lock of her naturally wavy strawberry-blond hair, and twisted it around her finger.

"So buy some sunscreen."

"If this is your bid for me to take on another case, take a look around, Brax." Abandoning the curl, she swept her hand over the collection of files and notes, and the stack of messages to be returned. "I'm up to my eyebrows in alligators, here. Three cases pending, and one court appearance."

"Are you turning down an opportunity to get back in the field?"

"I haven't been in the field—not like this, anyway— in months." The fact of the matter was, she hadn't been involved in a hands-on field investigation since her last and nearly disastrous case.

"Like riding a bicycle. You never forget how."

"I'm not sure—"

"I am."

He tossed another file onto her desk. "Suspected arson. The claim has already been paid."

"Great," Abby said, recognizing determination when she heard it. She pulled the file to her, and opened it. "Couldn't you have started me back off with an easy one?"

"Easy is boring."

"I could stand a little boredom."

"Like hell. You thrive on excitement."

That was before...

Quickly, Abby shoved the thought from her mind. She glanced up from the file, careful not to meet Brax's sharp-eyed gaze. He knew her too well to be fooled by false protestations to the contrary.

The truth was, she did thrive—or maybe *had* thrived was more appropriate—on the thrill of investigating an intriguing case, ferreting out information, uncovering facts and nailing the bad guys when the occasion called for it. Highly competitive and driven to succeed, she loved every compelling aspect of her job. Or was that *had* loved?

A year and a half ago she had paid a high price for that love. It had almost cost her everything. Including her hard-earned self-confidence, not to mention her self-respect. And lately she had been asking herself if her killer instincts were a thing of the past. More important, how did she feel if they were?

"And I suppose this is your idea of exciting?" She flipped the cover back and checked the date stamped in the upper right-hand corner. "It's over nine months old and a done deal. R.L.G." She pointed to the initials of the insurance company's investigator next to the date. "Gunderson, right?"

"Right."

"I know Rob and I'd be willing to bet he turned this case inside out."

"Yeah. And it looked clean."

"So?"

"So, we got a call from the insurance company this morning, who got a call from Seattle P.D. yesterday. Seems Seattle picked up a burglar—small-time, really—but he wants to cut a deal. They reduce the charges, and he gives them a guy that hired him to blow up a boat in Hawaii."

Abby glanced at the document stapled to the top sheet—a copy of a check in the amount of $232,000, made out to Gilbert C. Leland and Houston Sinclair, for a hull-coverage policy on a boat named, *Two of a Kind*. The mailing address was Lone Star Dive Shop & Tours, 600 Front Street, Lahaina, Maui, Hawaii.

"Maui," she interjected, still perusing the file. "Hawaii is the big island."

"Whatever."

"Brax—" she looked up from her reading "—you know as well as I do that perps spout off that kind of deal at the drop of a hat. Half the time it turns out to be bogus."

"Yeah, but the Seattle perp is an ex-navy demolitionist. And he says he rigged the boat to explode for this man—"

"Who probably gave him a false name."

"Didn't give him a name at all. This torch told him he was a friend of a friend. He received all his instructions over the phone, and all his money through the mail. But he did remember the name of the boat."

Pausing for effect, Brax grinned. "The *Two of a Kind.*"

Abby stopped reading, and tented her fingers over the open file.

She was interested, and he knew it. He always knew when he had her hooked. Only this time, she was feeling like a fish out of water.

She and Brax had started to work for Rinehart Insurance Investigators on the same day four years ago, he as a management trainee, she as an assistant investigator. Now he was a district manager. And she was—had been, and hoped to be again—senior investigator. They had worked hard to get where they were. Harder than most people knew. Their personal lives had suffered. How many dinners had Brax's wife kept warm while he worked late? How many of his kid's school plays had he missed? As for Abby, well . . . the kindest commentary on her personal life would be to say nothing, to forget she had ever had one.

Yes, they had come a long way. And both of them had the scars to prove it.

"Give me an overview," she said, finally.

"According to the file, Leland and Sinclair are a couple of charm boys with a taste for adventure. They're into fast cars and faster women. But they're not dummies. Leland was on the San Francisco police force for five years, and Sinclair was a pilot . . . in the navy," he said, pointing out the obvious connection between Sinclair and the ex-navy demolition expert.

Charm boys. Just what she needed.

"Not exactly your average criminal stereotypes," she admitted grudgingly.

"Yeah? Don't forget we've seen a couple of saintly grandmother types take insurance companies for big bucks."

"Okay, so there's cause to reopen. And *maybe* a possible connection between the torch and Sinclair."

"A strong 'maybe.'"

"Other suspects?"

"Sinclair and Leland own a dive shop. You know, whale-watch tours, scuba diving. That kind of stuff. According to the file, they have one full-time employee and a couple of part-timers. Some possibles there."

"What about debts, mistresses, et cetera? Owners or employees?"

"As for the partners, they're mostly debt free except for the boat that went up. The manager, a guy named Stuart Baker, is a drifter type. Came to work a few weeks before the explosion. Couple of part-time native divers. No records on any of them."

"They replace the boat they lost?"

"Oh, yeah. But this time they bought a much less expensive, reconditioned, used catamaran."

"Any idea what they did with the extra money?"

"They both said they intended to put it back into the business. Said it under oath, I might add."

Abby nodded. "Any ex-wives out to get even?"

"Leland was practically a newlywed, and Sinclair's never been married."

Abby checked the personal data form, and saw that Houston Sinclair was thirty-four. She wondered why he had never married. Not that it was out of the ordinary for a man to remain single into his thirties. Still, the answer might shed some light on a motive, since Sinclair would undoubtedly be on her list of suspects.

Who knows? Maybe the guy had a demanding babe on the side, and he needed money to keep her happy. She was doubtful the first investigator would have missed it, but it was possible.

"Nothing on any of the employees?"

"Zip. Clean as a whistle."

"Any reason someone would want the partners dead or framed for fraud?"

He shook his head. "I told you, Gunderson came up empty-handed."

Abby eyed her longtime friend and superior. "You think the partners are the culprits, don't you?"

"Call it a hunch. The torch says the bomb had a timer. Either one could have set it off."

"What about the connection between the torch and the money man? What about the friend of a friend?"

"Seattle is checking into it. But we've got an ex-navy pilot and an ex-navy demo man. We've got an ex-cop that could have God-knows-what kind of connections."

"I don't know, Brax. From what I can tell, there's not much in this file to support your hunch. If your suspicions are accurate, these two guys—" she gestured toward the copy of the check "—are serious arsonists."

"Assuming they were both in on the arson."

"Which is not a stretch, given the fact that they are partners." She flipped through the forms looking for background information. "Is their relationship long-standing? Personal or strictly business?"

"They've known each other since grade school."

Abby arched an eyebrow, and let the pages flop back into place. "I might buy a piece of your hunch if we can establish a strong enough motive. Any ideas?"

Brax shrugged. "Drugs. Blackmail. It could be anything. Hell, who knows? Maybe they just decided they wanted to downsize. In our business, stranger things have happened. That's what *you* need to find out, Miss Abigail."

"Gunderson didn't turn up any hard evidence?"

"There was nothing left of the boat. Not even a sliver that forensics could check. Sunk like the proverbial rock. Salvage yards were checked, but nothing turned up. Of course, wreckage has been known to turn up on beaches after a time, but as of now, we've got *nada.*"

"And this Sinclair survived?"

"Yeah, but he bobbed around in the Pacific for three days with a cut leg and raging fever, and didn't remember much."

"Or so he says." Abby picked up a pencil and began tapping it against the top of her desk. "And knowing how thorough Rob is, whoever is responsible must have done one helluva job covering their tracks." The more they talked, the more intrigued she became, yet at the same time, the more her instincts warned her to leave this one alone. Instincts, plus the nagging question of whether or not she had lost her edge.

"Obviously. When I spoke with Gunderson he admitted the partners were his first suspects, but he was never able to make a connection. As I said, they found nothing of the boat. No physical evidence of any kind. And as for the death of Leland's wife—"

"Wife?"

"She died in the explosion."

Abby lifted the copy of the check, for the first time noticing another copy behind it. A copy of a check in the amount of one hundred thousand dollars, paid to Gilbert Leland on a life-insurance policy on his wife.

"Maybe the torch wasn't after the partners at all. Maybe he was after the wife."

"Possible. But Sinclair's deposition indicates Mrs. Leland came along at the last minute. The husband confirms it. Doesn't look as if it was preplanned. The most important item as far as I'm concerned is that Leland increased the life-insurance policy three months after they were married," Brax continued.

"According to the file, all of the insurance was increased, including life on Mrs. Leland. Could be coincidence."

"Yeah, I could be way off base on this one. That's why I'm depending on you to do your usual excruciatingly thorough best. The insurance company got clipped for almost a half a mil on this one. We get the bad guys, then we get a nice chunk of change. So, I want 'em."

In the past she had been just as eager for the kill. But the old thrill of the chase wasn't zinging through her blood as usual. What Brax took for a thorough examination of the case was more a cover for her insecurity.

"I wonder why the insurance company didn't let Rob take up the case where he left off. He's a good investigator." She picked up the pencil, rolling it back and forth between her hands.

"You're better. And you're a good-looking woman."

"Flattery? Isn't that a sneak attack, even for you?"

"Not if it works."

"You should know by now that you can't flatter me, Brax."

"Why, Miss Abigail, don't you know?" He flashed her a cocky grin, knowing the nickname was not one she cherished. "You're long and leggy, and definitely easy on the eyes. And you're certainly one of the best, if not the best investigator I've got."

"Don't you mean, used to be?" She crossed and uncrossed the aforementioned long legs, irritated that the little insecurity had slipped out before she could stop herself.

His smile faded. "If that's what I meant, that's what I'd have said. You made a mistake, Abby, and you paid for it." He looked at her, and his usually stern expression softened. "Dearly, I might add. Personally and professionally."

Her gaze darted away, and she laid the pencil aside. "I'm okay."

"You are now."

And she was. But only because she had finally come to terms with the reality that she was fundamentally flawed.

She had a weakness for charming men.

And with one exception, Riley Waterston had been the most charming man she had ever known. At least at first. In the end, he had become as vicious as a rabid dog.

With startling clarity, Abby remembered only too well the day Riley had been arrested. The day he'd turned to her, and in a clear, emotionless voice had coldly informed her that she pretended a good game, but that was all she could do. She had looks, intelligence and ambition. But that was all. What she lacked was a woman's heart. A real woman's heart.

It had taken some tears and the perspective granted by time, but Abby had finally realized there was a grain of truth in Riley's words. She had spent a lifetime protecting her heart because she considered it traitorous, at best. Hearts were too fragile. Too easily broken. Particularly by fascinating men. It was a lesson Abby had learned at an early age.

Yes, she was okay now, but the road back had been long, dark and rough.

"I have to admit this case has snagged my interest," Abby said, shaking off thoughts of the gloomy past to concentrate on the present.

"I knew it would."

On the surface, the whole thing looked cut-and-dried: reinvestigation of a fraud. She had done dozens of them, but there was something about this one that made her hesitate. Maybe it was because a woman had been killed. It was horrific enough that the two suspects might have scammed the insurance company. But fraud was a far cry from murder—even accidental murder.

Or maybe it was because Sinclair and Leland looked to be cut from the same cloth as a certain smooth-talking man from her past. Or maybe she feared she had lost her nerve. Or all of the above.

Abby cleared her throat and picked up the pencil again, this time nervously tapping the eraser against the thick file.

She hadn't thought about Riley Waterston in over two months—something of a record, considering he had almost ended her career, not to mention the fact that he'd shredded her heart. Getting personally involved with a subject under investigation was considered a cardinal sin in her business. It was death to an investigator's objectivity.

It had been death to Abby's faith in love and herself. And the empty hole of loneliness inside her just got bigger and bigger.

But she had worked her way back with a new resolve, a new strength. And an impenetrable guard around her heart.

"Don't take this as a sexist remark, but you're the right woman for this job. To begin with, we need fresh eyes and instincts. Secondly, someone has to get close to these men. Know anybody better than a woman to get close to a man?"

Alarm bells went off in her head. Post-Riley alarms that warned against getting close under *any* circumstances. But she told herself she was a new woman, a much stronger woman. She could handle this.

"The job could be tough, but you've earned a chance to prove you can stand the heat, Abby. You walked back in here with your head high, and fought for the top spot. I think nailing this case will get you a promotion to senior investigator again.''

"That's some carrot you're waving under my nose."

"Is it working?"

She grinned. "You knew it would."

Brax grinned back. "Yeah."

Secretly he heaved a huge sigh of relief. To be honest, he had been scared to death that her experience with that sleazebag, Waterston, would stop her from ever taking on this kind of undercover investigation again. She had good cause to be leery of anything that put her in close contact with slick-talking, smooth-operating scam artists who knew every woman's secret fantasy, and played on them like Van Cliburn on a baby grand. She wasn't obligated to accept this assignment, and Brax wouldn't have thought any less of her if she had turned it down. The fact that she didn't reassured him. Abby might still be nursing a bruised heart, but she damned well wasn't going to let it ruin her career or her life.

"So when do I leave?"

"You're booked on a 6:52 flight tomorrow morning. A tourist out to enjoy her well-earned annual vacation."

"Sure of yourself, weren't you?"

He hedged the truth. "No. But I was sure of you."

"Well, let's just hope your instincts about this case are as reliable."

Long after Brax left her office Abby thought about this second chance she had just been given. A chance to do it right. To regain some of what she had lost. To use the lessons she had learned. Or relearned, to be more accurate.

This wasn't new ground for her. It was, in fact, a lesson learned from the first charming man in her life.

Her father.

Adam Douglass had been every little girl's dream. When he was home. Which was seldom. As a band manager he was always on the road. Always a long-distance daddy. Oh, but when he returned! Abby could still recall wonderful outings to the zoo, carnivals and picnics in the park. And the compliments. Her father never failed to tell her how smart she was. How beautiful. How proud he was of her.

Her mother came to life during those times. She smiled and laughed. Those were the happy times, happy days. The happiest of Abby's life.

And when he was gone, which was more often than not, Abby held tight to her memories. They sustained her from one homecoming to the next. Her mother, on the other hand, withered.

It was the only word Abby had ever found to successfully describe the transformation that occurred in her mother whenever her father left to go back on the road. It wasn't that Samantha Douglass wasn't a good mother. She was. She held down a low-paying but steady job as a clerk in a department store. She kept her only child clean and as well-fed as possible. Taught her right from wrong and the Ten Commandments.

But she was only going through the motions of living—merely surviving—without her husband. Samantha Douglass hung on his every spellbinding word. He was not only her lover and mate, he was her guide and counselor. In many ways he was as much her parent as he was Abby's. She viewed life apart from him as not only colorless, but frightening.

When Abby was fifteen, her father died of an unexpected heart attack. But she buried her mother. Emotionally, at least.

Adam Douglass had left the two women in his life two very different legacies. For Samantha, it was life without color or direction.

For Abby, it was happy memories of a doting father. And the certain knowledge that charming men were transient. They came and they went. But they never stayed.

For years after her father's death, Abby tried to bring some sparkle into her mother's life. She worked hard to be the brightest, the smartest—the best at everything. But it didn't work. It was only after she was old enough to fall in love for the first time that Abby realized that her mother wasn't grieving; she had given up. Everything in her mother's life had revolved around her father. Without him, she didn't have a life.

Abby made a promise to herself that no man, captivating or not, would ever control her life that way.

Riley Waterston and his devastating charm had come close to making her forget that promise. And had made her break the rules.

There were certain unwritten rules that went with her job. Certain rules every investigator acknowledged. Rules designed to protect people like Abby—good at their job because they knew how to play the games required to catch liars, thieves, arsonists, extortionists and even murderers.

In the world of lawyers and courts, suspects were presumed innocent until proved guilty. In Abby's world, none of the suspects was presumed innocent until each one was systematically eliminated, leaving the last person guilty—with plenty of hard evidence as proof—standing alone to face the consequences.

The rules were simple.

Never trust a suspect until he or she is duly eliminated.

Never assume any piece of evidence, no matter how small, is inconsequential.

Never count on a piece of evidence without adequate verification.

Never forget your loyalty is to the company.

And never, never lose your objectivity.

Abby broke the rules. Specifically, two.

She had trusted Riley Waterston too quickly. And she had lost her objectivity.

Abby could remember all too well how easy it had been to break those rules. How easily she had fallen into his well-placed trap.

He'd told her what she wanted to hear. What every woman wanted to hear. But not the usual compliments on her beauty, grace and charm. Oh, no, Riley was far too clever to be so mundane. He told her she was smart, and talented. All the wonderful words her father had always used. Words she couldn't resist. But most of all he praised her ability to be a hard-working, intelligent woman while still retaining every bit of her femininity. He told her that he admired her, and that she touched him as no woman ever had.

What woman wouldn't go for that like a cat goes for cream?

But Abby knew it was much more than falling under the influence of some pretty words. Riley Waterston was good at beguiling and spellbinding; maybe the best she had ever seen. And she had fallen like a ripe plum. But what worried Abby was not that she had fallen, but that she had fallen so hard and completely, and in the process had lost all her objectivity.

The loss of her objectivity—not merely succumbing to soft-spoken words—frightened her, rocked her to her foundation.

She had been attracted to investigation targets before. After all, she wasn't made of marble. But none of them had gotten to her the way Riley had. He had a knack for finding out her heart's desire, then holding out that very desire to her like some shining golden dream that was hers for the taking. And she had taken the bait like a big fat bass after spinner bait, swallowing it, hook, line and sinker. He had kept her on the hook, never completely reeling her in. He had fed her one false lead after another, all designed to make her believe his cooperation stemmed from an honest desire to help her find the guilty party.

Riley Waterston had assaulted her, professionally and personally, as surely as if he had used his fists.

Professionally, he had made her someone to be pitied. It had taken her long months of doing her job better than anyone in the department, of putting on a smile when she felt like crying, to overcome the damage left in Riley's wake.

Personally, he had wounded her spirit as surely as if he had taken a knife to her heart—the heart she wasn't supposed to have.

Abby had a near miss with Riley and now she was being handed a second chance. She couldn't afford to make the same mistake twice.

Chapter 2

Hands shoved deep in the pockets of his jeans, his face to the wind, Houston Sinclair watched the sun rise over the water, and a yearning so deep, so bittersweet, pierced his heart that his breath caught. Lahaina's small boat harbor was teeming with life even at this early hour, and he longed to be a part of the activity. But longing, no matter how earnest, didn't always ensure reality. For Houston reality was standing onshore and watching. Only watching.

He couldn't go back in—or on—the water.

Heaving a soul-weary sigh, he wondered if his particular reality would ever change.

Almost nine months had passed since the Coast Guard had hauled him out of the Pacific, unconscious, feverish and delirious.

And alone.

He had put his life back in order as best as he could. He had even been semisuccessful at pretending that this fear—no, this gut-level, unadulterated *terror*—wasn't gnawing at his insides like some flesh-eating insect. Nine months. And a lot of that time had been spent very much the same way he was spending this morning: feeling tense and haunted.

These post-dawn watches were always the result of a sleepless night. But when he did sleep, the nightmares robbed him of even that freedom from torment. Tortured dreams in which he relived the explosion. Relived his only clear pieces of memory.

Two pieces. They were short; only seconds, really. In the first, he heard Shelley call out for him and he turned from her voice. In the second, he helplessly watched the *Two of a Kind* sink.

But nightmares notwithstanding, even his dreams weren't peaceful. Often in his dreams he saved his best friend's wife only to lose her to sharks, or, as in one bizarre dream segment, she simply slipped over the side and swam away, finally disappearing with a gentle wave of her hand. In all the dreams, all the nightmares, the end result was the same—he was alone, and Shelley was dead.

He could deal with the dreams, even the nightmares, but not the memories. Memories that crept to the edge of his mind like morning fog over San Francisco Bay, then clung to his subconscious, never fully realized. Memories always just out of reach, tucked away in the darkness, waiting. Did they hold absolution? Or confirmation of his cowardice?

"Traumatic memory loss," the doctor who had treated him had called it, assuring him that in time he would remember. The problem was, Houston didn't want to remember. Even the bits and pieces of memory he could claim ripped at his guilt, his sanity.

If it had not been for Gil . . .

Gil. His friend. His lifeline.

The first person he saw when he opened his eyes after the ordeal was Gil, teary-eyed, saying everything was going to be all right. Saying he knew Houston had done everything in his power to save Shelley. Gil, saying over and over how glad he was to still have his best friend. Gil, watching over him, sticking by him.

Forgiving him.

And it was the forgiveness Houston couldn't live with, because he didn't deserve it.

No matter how many times Gil insisted that what had happened was a freak accident, totally out of anyone's control, Houston knew the truth.

It was his fault.

Shelley was dead because he was a coward.

If he had gone for her first. If only...

He closed his eyes. The *if only*s were driving him to the brink of insanity.

Slowly, he opened his eyes and glanced down, half expecting to see the toes of his shoes sticking over the edge of some black abyss. Or half disappointed? He couldn't deny that once in a while the idea of stepping over the mental edge sounded almost comforting. A tight laugh tangled with a sigh of relief when he realized the absurd bent his imagination had taken. He kicked at a pebble. It rolled across the wooden dock and over the edge, and plopped into the water.

No, there was no way to avoid the responsibility of what he had done. The biggest question in Houston's mind was not how to avoid it, but how to live with it. For three days he had drifted in the Pacific like so much flotsam and jetsam. Three days in the water, waiting to die, expecting to die. But he hadn't.

Now he had to live with his shame.

Ever since the accident he had tried with only moderate success to steer his life into the wind, back on course. Out there in the ocean he had been physically adrift. Now he was emotionally adrift, as well.

Houston turned his back on the ocean he loved so much, and headed toward Front Street.

The moment he unlocked the back door to Lone Star Dive Shop & Tours he smelled fresh coffee brewing. "Gil?" he called out, pocketing his key.

"Yo!" came the response from the upstairs office.

Houston climbed the narrow stairs to find his partner bent over an open accounts ledger. "You know, if you'd cook those damned books," he teased, pouring himself a cup of the steaming brew, "you wouldn't have to work so hard."

"Hey, it's hard enough to keep one set balanced. I'm not smart enough to cheat." Gil Leland eyed the dark circles under Houston's eyes and didn't have to make much of an educated guess about where he had been.

"Been down by the harbor again?"

Houston nodded, giving the act of sipping his coffee more attention than it deserved.

"I think you ought to stay away from there."

When Houston laughed out loud, Gil realized the irony of his statement. "Look, you'll get past this. It may take some time, but you *will* make it through to the other side."

"And in the meantime you and Stuart have got to handle all the dives and whale watches. All the sunset cruises, all the charters..." He pointed to the ledger. "And you're still doing the accounts, just like always. It's not fair, Gil."

"What the hell does 'fair' have to do with anything? What's *fair* about any of this?"

Houston turned to face his partner. "How do you do it?"

"What? Make it through the day without crying? Keep on going when sometimes I'd like to find a deep hole somewhere, and jump in?"

"Yeah."

Their discussions about the accident, and how each of them was dealing with their grief were cyclical. When one of them was down, the other always seemed to be up enough to help. Despite the doctor's recommendation that Houston see a psychotherapist, Gil was the only person he had been able to talk to about what had happened.

"I couldn't do it without you," Gil said softly.

"Me? Hell, I'm an albatross around your neck. I'm—"

"Just knock it off, Sinclair."

Houston's mouth opened to say something, then he thought better of it. Whenever Gil referred to him as "Sinclair," he knew the ex-cop had something serious to say.

"Last week you found me crying in my beer. Literally. You told me Shelley would have been hopping mad to see me that way, and you were right. Well, right back atcha. You know what she would say if she were standing here now? She'd put her hands on her hips, and take that now-you-listen-here-buster stance that told you you were about to get both barrels of whatever she was unloading. Remember?"

Houston couldn't help but grin, remembering Shelley's spitfire personality and envisioning the exact pose Gil had just described so accurately.

"Then she'd crank up her Alabama accent a couple of notches, and tell you to get that 'hangdawg look off your face,' or she was 'gonna box your ears.' And I believe," Gil said, closing the ledger, "that's a direct quote."

"I believe you're right."

"My point," Gil offered, rising from the desk with his coffee cup in his hand, "is that she wouldn't want you turning yourself inside out over something that wasn't your fault. Neither do I." He held up his hand to forestall the rebuttal he knew was on the tip of Houston's tongue. "And before you comment about those minor repairs on the boat, don't forget that I knew about them, too. I could have insisted they be fixed. I didn't because they were minor. *Minor*. Nobody, and I mean *nobody,* had any way of knowing the damn propane fuel line had a leak." Gil poured himself more coffee.

"We don't know that's what caused the explosion," Houston commented, even though result, not reason, was what mattered to him.

"What else could it have been? At sunset Shelley went down to the galley to make a pot of coffee. It was sort of a tradition with her. Anytime she was on the boat at that hour, she made coffee."

"If only I hadn't—"

"If, if, if. You've got to stop doing this to yourself. To both of us," Gil added after a long pause.

"I'm sorry," Houston said, feeling more guilt and shame than ever for not setting Gil straight about why he blamed himself. A week before the accident some minor repairs had needed to be made, but hadn't been done. Then Shelley had insisted on coming along at the last minute. And finally, a young couple having trouble with the motor on their sailboat had waved them down for assistance. If they hadn't stopped to help, the *Two of a Kind* would have been docked in Hilo before sunset, and Shelley wouldn't have gone below to make coffee.

All of which was true. All of which didn't matter when stacked up against the fact that his shame was made twofold by allowing Gil to believe a lie.

"Hey," Gil said, trying to lighten the mood. "Stuart tells me he's got an all-female snorkel-and-dive set up this morning. Taking all six of them out to Molokini."

"Probably middle-aged, old-maid schoolteachers looking for some—" Houston raised the first two fingers of each hand and made quotes in the air "—'real adventure.'"

Gil laughed.

"By the way," Houston said, grateful for the change of subject, "I owe you an apology about Stuart. You know I wasn't much in favor of hiring him at first, but I was wrong. He's good help."

"See there, slick," he said, referring to the tag hung on Houston during their high-school days when he had been one of the smoothest, slickest receivers in the state. "I told you my instincts about him were right on the money."

"But even you have to admit, trusting your instincts without doing much checking into his background is not the ideal way to hire someone."

"Worked out, didn't it? Stuart's a little moody now and then, and he damned sure isn't much of a conversationalist, but he knows the business, and he's steady."

"Agreed. You were right, and I was wrong."

"Aha. Music to my ears." Gil slapped Houston on the back. "Let's go down and see if Stuart's schoolmarms have arrived. Betcha five dollars there's not one out of the six under forty or without glasses."

"You're on."

When they got downstairs Houston and Gil took one look at the women gathered around the counter, and agreed that if they weren't schoolteachers, they should have been. A couple were signing liability release forms while the three others chatted, applying sunscreen to each other's pale arms and backs. All were dressed in one-piece bathing suits that might have stood a remote chance of being labeled risqué in the fifties.

Gil turned to Houston. "Pay up."

"I only count five. No money exchanges hands until Miss Six shows up."

At that moment the front door opened, and in walked a woman that could never be mistaken for an old maid. And if she was a schoolteacher, Houston decided he could use a refresher course. The subject didn't matter.

She was tall, with legs clear up to forever, and the rest of her wasn't bad, either. A skimpy, aquamarine two-piece bathing suit showed off a well-toned body that could easily have been labeled risqué. Not the hard, exercise-produced kind of firmness, but the sleek, smooth curves of a real woman. Her skin had a light golden base tan that spoke of recent trips to a tanning salon. Smart, too, he thought. Smart enough to know a good base tan, even for skin as fair as hers, could be the difference between a miserable sunburn and a pleasant vacation. And he liked the way she carried herself— with poise, confidence.

If this was Miss Six, and he certainly hoped so, he was about to win the bet.

Houston stepped around the counter. "Can I help you?"

"Yes." She removed her sunglasses to reveal a pair of bright blue eyes sparkling like sunlight on the Pacific.

"My name is Abigail Douglass," she said, her voice soft, sultry. As she switched the glasses to her left hand and extended her right hand for him to shake, she looked straight into his eyes. "I booked a dive for today."

Taking her hand, the first thought that popped into Houston's head was that she was a triple threat: stunning eyes, seductive voice and incredibly soft skin.

Gazing into those gorgeous blue eyes, he suddenly wondered what she would do if he slipped his hand up her soft, bare arm and shoulder to stroke her neck; to slightly tilt her head back. Would her lips part in surprise? Would she—

"Uh, yes, Ms. Douglass," Houston said, yanking himself back to the business at hand. He dropped her hand a little too quickly, considering he felt as if he had been holding it for hours. This sort of blatant fantasizing wasn't like him at all. But then, Abigail Douglass wasn't like anyone he had met in a long time.

He glanced at her left hand, and was relieved to find it bare of rings. On a second glance, he noticed a small mesh dive bag containing flippers and a regulator hanging from her shoulder.

"I take it this isn't your first dive?"

"No, but I'm still a novice."

The first thought that popped into Abby's head when she looked into Houston Sinclair's dark brown eyes was that he was wickedly handsome. As in, handsome as sin. As in, the kind of man your mother had always warned you about. And the kind you had always secretly wanted to meet.

Tall, tanned and broad-shouldered, he had the kind of body that was toned from work, not workouts.

Yes, he was good-looking. She'd give him that. And she had to admit that she liked his beard. And his mustache. Both were neatly trimmed to outline his mouth and jaw. Very sexy. The ladies undoubtedly went for it, big time. The same went for the tiny gold hoop earring in his left earlobe. A little piratical flair. Very sexy, indeed. But then, judging from his confident appraisal of her, Abby figured he was not totally unaware of his appeal.

"Where have you been diving?"

"Cozumel a couple of times. Once to Aruba, and once to Grand Cayman."

Abby could see that her plan—"the plan," Brax had called it—was working. Sinclair was interested in her. And his interest would make her job that much easier. But at the moment, her job wasn't uppermost in her mind. Not with Houston looking at her so intently.

"Cayman is always gorgeous." And so was she. Houston couldn't keep his eyes off her. He couldn't remember when he had been so completely attracted, so quickly.

"I don't dive as much as I would like," Abby said. "But I do love it."

"It's an addiction."

"You're probably right. I know I'd hate like the devil to give up anything I love this much." Her steady gaze held his. "Diving gives me a feeling of being in my own private world filled with color and life. Yeah, you might say I'm addicted."

As Houston had been. Once. In fact, Abigail Douglass had just perfectly expressed his own sentiments about diving.

"Well." Damn, but her eyes were beautiful. "I'm sure you'll enjoy Molokini, it's breathtaking. Since you're the only one in this group diving, we've arranged for a group from the Maui Dive Shop to join us. Stuart—" he nodded toward the man behind the counter "—is an excellent dive master."

"You're not certified?"

"Yes. We…take turns. Gil is doing the whale watch this afternoon. Stuart is taking out your group."

"Oh."

Was that disappointment he heard in her voice? A secret little thrill shot through Houston until he realized how truly disappointed this woman would be if she knew the truth. That he couldn't dive. Couldn't even go swimming.

"Guess this is old hat to you. Living in paradise, you can dive any time you want to." Abby was picking up some negative vibes from Sinclair. Like maybe he had something to hide?

"Yeah," Houston said, hoping the anxiety tightening his gut wasn't detectable in his voice.

"At least you don't have to worry about vacationer's syndrome."

"Vacationer's syndrome?"

"I'm told you don't actually get it until your last day here. Probably when you start to pack. After all this sunshine, balmy breezes and tropical beauty, you have to face going home to the plain old, everyday world." She wrinkled her nose. "Vacation's over. Having to give it up is worse than never having it at all, don't you think?"

Much worse, he thought, recalling his love of the sea.

"So, how long is your vacation?" Houston asked, wanting to move away from the subject of giving up things one loved.

Abby closed her eyes, smiling. "Ten glorious days. And I'm afraid I've already been bitten by the bug."

"Are you staying in Maui the whole time?"

She opened her eyes, and again met his gaze directly. Man-to-woman directly. "That depends."

Houston's reaction was immediate and purely physical. He was not without experience when it came to playing the game of verbally feeling each other out. He knew interest when he saw it, and this woman was telling him in no uncertain terms that she was interested.

And surprisingly enough, although his reaction was definitely physical, his interest went deeper. Perhaps it had to do with her statement about giving up things one loved, or the way those intelligent-looking blue eyes gazed back at him. Whatever the reason, he wanted to see more of Abigail Douglass. A lot more.

"It's a beautiful island. Lots to see, and do. I hope you'll stick around, and dive with us again."

"I just may do that," she said softly. "Thanks, Mr.—"

"Sinclair, but call me Houston, please."

"All right. Thanks, Houston."

"My pleasure," he said, as she walked over to join the other women standing by the front door. A second later Stuart herded them out the door and toward the docks.

Gil, who had been watching the exchange, walked up to Houston and handed him a five-dollar bill. "Here you go, slick. Never let it be said I don't pay my gambling debts."

Houston glanced down at the bill. "Keep your money." He walked to the front and looked out at the group making their way through the tourists and shoppers. As he watched Abigail Douglass walk away, Houston experienced a surge of hope. It washed over him like a tidal wave.

And he felt more alive than he had in nine long months.

Chapter 3

She hadn't expected Houston Sinclair to be so warm and charming. Or so good-looking. That neatly trimmed beard and mustache of his was definitely dashing.

Not that it mattered in the grand scheme of things, Abby reminded herself, standing at the bow pulpit of the catamaran as it skimmed over the turquoise-blue ocean toward the inlet of Molokini. Not that it mattered one bit where her plan was concerned. His charm and looks had nothing to do with her investigation, other than the fact that she now knew how to handle charming, good-looking men who were also suspects. She handled them the same way anyone would handle a potentially dangerous virus they had been exposed to: take appropriate measures to protect yourself, and keep your distance.

And Abby considered herself well protected. Hadn't she been inoculated against this particular virus by Dr. "Charm" Waterston himself? Oh, she'd had it bad, all right. So bad, in fact, that she had almost let a guilty man go free. Almost let a lying, cheating, manipulating con artist get away with nearly a million dollars of the company's money.

Abby shivered, thinking how close she had come to letting Riley go scot-free. What a fool she had been! What an utter fool. How could she have believed all his lies?

The answer was simple. So simple, it was hard to accept.

Her fundamental flaw. A weakness she couldn't afford. The same kind of weakness that had reduced her mother to a dull, dreary life. The kind of weakness she must guard against—no matter the cost.

Abby sighed, disgusted with herself for dwelling on a past she couldn't change. She had learned her lesson. And she had learned how to hide her fundamental flaw behind ambition and a single-minded drive to be the best at everything she did. She wouldn't make the same mistake her mother had made.

And she wasn't about to allow Houston Sinclair to get to her, even if he did drip charm like maple-tree sap.

Since she had to play out the scenario of tourist in order for her plan to be convincing, Abby decided it was much too beautiful a day to dwell on the past. She had a dazzling blue sky, and the treasures of an azure sea waiting to be enjoyed.

Molokini, a favorite dive destination, was a crescent-shaped remnant of an exposed volcanic crater. Three miles off the south coast of Maui, the uninhabited land mass was a marine preserve abounding in tropical fish and calm waters.

As the catamaran dropped anchor, Abby leaned over from the dive platform and dipped her buoyancy-control vest into the water. Then she began the time-consuming but necessary-for-survival, step-by-step procedures every diver must do in order to enjoy the sport and live to enjoy it again. After attaching her tank to the B.C., then connecting the octopus to her tank and the air-supply hose to her B.C., she strapped her regulator in place. Seated at the edge of the dive platform facing in, her mask defogged, her knife strapped to her calf, Abby put on her vest, fins, weights and mask, then fitted the regulator in her mouth and tumbled backward into the sea.

She surfaced immediately, gave the "okay" signal to Stuart Baker, and set her dive watch. Then she waited for the divers from the Maui Dive Shop boat, anchored a couple of hundred yards away, to join her. Stuart followed her into the water a few moments later. Once the four other divers had arrived, Stuart and Abby raised their control hoses over their heads, pressed their air-escape values, and began their descents.

As always, Abby's first few seconds underwater were a mixture of anxiety, thrills and awe, then faded to a steady sense of watchful wonder. She descended, slowly turning her body in continuous circles until she reached a depth of approximately thirty-five feet. Off to her left, Stuart floated at zero buoyancy, maintaining his depth while videotaping the scenery and divers.

Enthralled and fascinated by the undersea world, Abby, too, hung at zero buoyancy for several minutes, allowing herself the pure pleasure of luxuriating in the beauty and color surrounding her. Sea turtles, a dozen or more, dotted the reef below, along with schools of parrot fish and an occasional manta ray. Off to her right, two turtles in particular snagged her attention as they swam, almost soaring through the water, flippers outstretched like wings. The larger of the two banked left, then landed on the reef. The other swam on.

As Abby watched the turtle settle atop an outcropping of coral not twenty-five feet from her, she caught

a movement in her peripheral vision. Stuart was frantically pointing to something over her left shoulder.
Abby turned.

And saw a shark coming straight at her.

Shark! Shark! The silent scream ricocheted through
her mind.

Part of her—the desperate part—wanted to race for
the surface. Run! Swim! Get away! her mind shrieked.
Another part—the saner part—demanded that she do
nothing to attract his attention. Don't move. Don't
breathe, reason insisted.

Reason won out at about the same instant long hours
of training kicked in. Abby froze, gasped a breath, and
held it. Her heart hammered so wildly in her chest, she
was sure her skin was moving; sure the shark would
mistake the movement for a distressed fish.

The shark kept coming.

She didn't dare move. Even though his eyesight might
be infinitely poor, the shark would zero in on the
slightest bit of motion. But she couldn't just hang there
and do nothing, like a piece of meat waiting for the
butcher. *He's coming straight at me, for God's sake.*

As cautiously as she could with every ounce of self-
preservation instinct pumping massive spurts of adrenaline through her bloodstream, Abby reached for her
knife. Her hand trembled as she fumbled with the Vel-
cro holding it in place. Finally, after seconds that
seemed like days, she pulled the knife out of its sheath
and held it up in front of her.

The shark kept coming.

She stared at the object of her fear, looming larger
and larger, like a deadly missile aimed right at her heart.
Its conical-shaped head and sleek body appeared almost still except for the powerful tail that swept back
and forth in the water. Back and forth. Bringing him
closer and closer. But in no great hurry. As if he knew

his leisurely approach would undermine her courage as nothing else would.

And it did. Terror vibrated through every cell of her body. Every muscle shrieked for her to obey its command to move. "Fight or flight" was no longer a concept on some printed page. It was real. It was now. *Don't move. Don't . . . don't . . .*

He was only a few feet away. Close enough—*Dear God*—for her to see—*save me*—rows and rows—*oh, please*—of sharp, white teeth. *Dear God . . .*

She closed her eyes and prayed. . . .

The shark bumped into her tank.

Her heart almost stopped. She opened her eyes in time to see him make a turn and swim toward her again.

He bumped her a second time. On her leg.

At the feel of his sandpaper-like skin lightly scraping hers, Abby stifled a scream by biting down so hard on her mouthpiece, she expected it to snap in two.

The shark turned away. Swam off to her right.

Then he turned back.

Headed straight for her again.

Only this time she knew it wouldn't be to test. This time it would be to taste.

Before she could raise the knife in her hand, without warning or provocation, abruptly the shark veered slightly to his right.

And silently cruised past her.

As all twelve or thirteen feet of the tiger shark slowly swam by her, Abby counted the reminder of her life in seconds. As she saw the cold, dead-looking eye, she waited for a lightning-fast change of direction. As she saw the dull gray skin move past close enough to touch, she waited for the razor-sharp teeth and powerful jaws to claim their first taste.

But when it came, she wasn't the victim.

In a move so fast, Abby would later question whether
or not she'd actually seen it, the shark made a hard left
turn, dove straight down toward the reef, and attacked
the turtle. Holding a flipper clamped in his massive
jaws, the shark thrashed his head back and forth. The
turtle struggled. The shark continued the vicious
thrashing. Then, miraculously, the turtle twisted free
and dove sideways between towers of coral too close
together for the shark to follow.

Abby gulped a huge lungful of air, releasing a giant
spray of bubbles.

The shark turned toward the sound.

Again, she froze. Held her breath. The bubbles
stopped.

No! No!

Once the bubbles disappeared, the shark, obviously
more interested in immediate prey, made a couple of
passes over the top of the turtle's coral hideout, then
simply swam away.

Slowly, Abby swigged air into her lungs as if she were
drinking from a thin straw. A thin line of bubbles escaped. She glanced around. Sharks were notorious for
swimming away, only to make a wide loop and return
for another go at their prey. She twisted her body in a
360-degree turn.

And discovered she was the only diver at that depth!

Before her panic level could shoot sky-high, she
looked up and saw Stuart, with a speargun in his hand,
swimming hard toward her.

Thank God! Thank God!

When he reached her, he gave Abby the sign to head
for the surface. He hung back, scanning the area for the
shark as he followed her up. The other divers were already out of the water.

Since decompression wasn't necessary at that depth,
Abby headed straight for the surface, all the while

turning, watching, expecting. On the surface, at the height of vulnerability, she clutched at the outstretched hands of the other divers as they yanked her out of the water and onto the deck.

Within minutes the boat streaked across the water to the spot where the ladies and Lonnie, a native diver and lifeguard, had been dropped off to snorkel. With a warning that a shark was possibly nearby, Stuart had no trouble collecting his charges in quick order. He then returned the Maui Dive Shop customers to their boat, then headed for another snorkel location.

But when they arrived at a peaceful-looking spot near the south end of Maui, Abby didn't want to snorkel. She didn't want to get back into the water.

She couldn't get back in the water now. Maybe never.

An hour later—the longest hour of her life—she sat at the very back of the boat, huddled under her terry-cloth beach cover like a child trying to hide from a big bad thunderstorm.

It was quiet except for the other women clustered around a stationary dining table twenty or so feet away, talking quietly. But when Abby had first climbed back on board she had been surrounded with questions from the other divers. Talking, talking, talking, when all she wanted to do was scream for them to shut up.

What did she think when she first saw the shark?

How close did he get?

How big was he?

How close was she to the turtle?

Did she think the shark was coming for her next?

Why didn't she use her knife?

Abby's wide-eyed gaze had darted from one man's face to another's, seeing their excitement, their...*envy!*

My God, she could have been killed. Tiger sharks had a nasty reputation, and were known to be almost as vicious as great whites. The beast had been twice her height in length and these...these *idiots* wanted to participate vicariously in her horrifying experience. Rage and gut-level terror rolled around together into a hard, snarled ball of resentment. For an instant Abby thought she *was* going to scream.

Men! She hated them. She hated their thirst for adventure and their need to reassert their macho egos with conquests. Killing sharks or seducing women. It was all the same to them.

She wanted to slap their faces—all of them. Or at the very least, shake some sense into them.

Luckily, she didn't have to resort to violence, because Stuart Baker stepped in and fended off the eager divers.

What was it with men and thrill-seeking? Abby wondered, staring out over the water from her little corner of safety. Most of them seemed to be drawn to it like weak minds to Svengali. Did they derive some sort of primeval adrenaline from heart-stopping, hair-raising encounters? Some addictive rush long since tamed into more civilized channels? Was that why they bungee jumped, drove fast cars even faster and did every daredevil thing known to mankind?

And they approached their relationships with women in the same way. It didn't matter that the methods used to conquer, subdue, gain mastery over, were soft words, whispered promises and seductive kisses. The end result was the same.

Abby took a deep, calming breath and realized she was mentally ranting. Raving, actually; directing every bit of her rage toward the unsuspecting male divers, when in actuality the bottom line, the very gut-level bottom line, was...

She was scared. No, terrified. Still.

Terrified deep down inside herself where such fears lived, waiting for the moment to erupt like some emotional volcano, spewing nightmarish phobias like hot lava.

She looked out over the water. Blue waves. Deep, dark waves... The thought of those waves, even with breathing equipment, closing over her head, her body, made Abby's heart rate skip to a rapid-fire count. Despite the terry-cloth cover-up, she actually felt her body break out in a cold sweat. Despite the wad of fabric she clutched in a death grip, her hand shook.

No. No, she couldn't go back in the water. Not now. Not any time soon. Maybe never.

Sadness, heavy and cloying, settled around her heart. She loved the ocean. Her infrequent but much-prized trips to any place with sparkling white beaches and turquoise waters were red-letter days on her calendar. The beauty and majesty of the sea had always been a love of her heart. To give it up was unthinkable.

But if she were forced to choose at this very moment, Abby knew she would walk away without a backward glance. So great was her fear.

She told herself it would take time to recover from such a terrifying encounter. She told herself it would pass; she would be fine. But no matter how much she reassured herself, Abby knew that dealing with her fear wasn't going to be easy or simple. The encounter with the shark had ripped away the thin veil of self-possessed security average human beings used to make it through a day without dying of fright; without cowering in the corners of their minds in abject terror. Her veil was gone. She felt exposed. Dangerously naked. Unarmed and undefendable.

She told herself she was being silly. She told herself to get it together, and get on down the road.

But by the time the catamaran docked, she was only moderately successful. She was still shaking, and the instant the boat was secured, tears gathered in her eyes.

Oh, no, she thought.

She was going to fall apart right here in front of the other women and Stuart's young native assistant. In front of the group of laughing young people everyone called "water babies," who practically lived on the docks. In front of God and everybody.

"Miz Douglass?"

She jumped at the sound of Stuart Baker's voice.

"Sent your tanks and stuff on ahead with Lonnie. Hope that's okay."

"What?" Abby glanced around, and realized everyone else was gone. Only she and the dive master remained, and he was looking at her. Staring, actually. Not that she hadn't been stared at by a number of men. Handsome men, at least. But Stuart Baker had an unfriendly, odd-looking face. His eyes didn't seem to be a good fit for the shape of his head, and his face was much too narrow for the shape of his mouth. He looked like a jigsaw puzzle gone bad.

"Just didn't think you'd..." Nervously, he glanced away and began coiling the anchor rope. "No reason you should hafta tote your stuff when Lonnie's back is strong enough to carry ten tanks. You can pick it up at the shop."

"Y-yes," she said, but didn't move.

After several seconds passed and she still hadn't moved, Stuart set aside the rope. He watched her, studied her face and her ramrod-stiff posture.

"Take a deep breath," he gently commanded.

Abby complied without thinking.

"Now another. And another."

She breathed deep, but too fast.

"Whoa. Blow the air out slowly."

She did, and gradually felt better. "Thanks," she whispered. Her cheeks felt hot—from anxiety or embarrassment, she couldn't say—and her heartbeat had gone from wildly thumping to merely galloping.

"I know grown men that wouldn't have done as well as you did today. You're a gutsy lady."

She looked into his eyes, and recognized not only sympathy, but compassion. Compassion born of experience? "I don't feel very gutsy."

He grinned, and she was astonished to see the change. All the pieces of the puzzle suddenly fell into place. His face became symmetrically balanced. Almost handsome.

"No. I imagine you feel like your heart's still beating like a runaway train and your legs are made out of water."

"That's putting it mildly."

At the mention of water Abby looked over the side of the boat. A narrow gangplank extended three or four feet from the boat to the dock. From her point of view it looked twenty feet long and two inches wide. And the water beneath it looked deep and deadly.

She turned to find Stuart staring at her once more, his face again misaligned. Her hands started to shake again.

"I—I'm . . . I'm not sure I can go b-back in the water again. Ever," she finished on a shaky breath.

There. She had said it out loud. She hadn't intended to or wanted to. The words had just come out. She was embarrassed and relieved at the same time.

"Got a right to your feelings," he said, almost as if he knew what it had cost her to speak the words. "Got a right to decide what's best for you."

Now she was shocked. When the day began she would never have classified the rugged dive master as sensitive, much less intuitive. To her amazement, he was both.

"Y-you don't think I'm overreacting?"

"Miz Douglass, you swam practically eyeball-to-eyeball with a tiger shark today. Nasty business, any way you cut it. You're shook, and you got a right to be. Any diver tells me he ain't gut-level scared of meeting a shark in open water—especially one that's bigger than him—is lying." He bobbed his chin as if to say, So there. "You're not overreacting."

Now she was ashamed. She had unintentionally included Stuart in her mental ravings against men. Abby almost felt the need to apologize.

He walked to the gangplank, turned, and held out a hand to assist her. She took it. Gladly, gratefully, allowing him to guide her across to dry land.

He didn't hold her hand a minute longer than he had to. A minute longer than she needed him to.

"Thank you very—"

"Don't wait on me." He nodded in the direction of Front Street. "Got work to do."

Abby took several steps before it dawned on her that he was giving her time to be alone. To compose herself. To regain her balance. She turned, intending to thank him again, but he was already at his task.

By the time she walked back into the Lone Star Dive Shop she was calmer. Not calm, but calmer.

"You're a star," Houston said, the minute she came through the door.

Leaning against the counter, he jerked a thumb toward the other side of the store. Gil Leland, Lonnie and the snorkel ladies were all gathered around a television set.

Abby frowned. "S-star?"

"They're playing the videotape."

"Tape?"

"The shark."

At that moment, the dive master and four divers from the Maui Dive Shop walked in. They immediately asked to view the tape.

"See what I mean," Houston said.

He watched her watching the faces of the people viewing her encounter.

She glanced from them to him. "They're watching it over and over."

"You've seen it?"

She shook her head.

"Want to?"

Did she? Wasn't living the experience enough? Why put herself through the horror twice?

Then again, maybe watching it wouldn't be as bad as she thought it would. Maybe seeing it from a different, that is to say, distant, perspective would help her deal with her fear.

"Have you seen it?" she asked.

He shook his head.

She swallowed hard, waiting. For what, she wasn't sure. Maybe for her nerves to stop jangling. Or for him to hold her hand. Neither was likely. So, she did the only thing she could. The only thing her pride permitted her to do. She faced her fear. She faced it scared, but she faced it.

Houston watched her gather her courage from some place deep inside herself. He actually saw her shoulders straighten, her chin tilt at just the slightest bit of a defiant angle.

"Maybe I'd better make sure I get star billing."

She did the best she could to smile. Under the circumstances, she did a damned fine job. A good enough job to make Houston want to reach for her hand, tell her he was proud of her.

Instead, he simply walked behind her toward the crowd of viewers.

"Hey," one of the divers said. "There she is. Our hero."

"Heroine," someone corrected him.

Everyone applauded. Houston thought he saw her blush, but he wasn't sure.

"Oh, it's so exciting," one of the snorkel ladies gushed.

Another agreed. "Absolutely. I can't wait to show my friends back in Tucson."

"Show?"

"We all bought copies of the video," a third chimed in.

"There," the visiting dive master called. "No. Wait. You went past it. Rewind."

Abby stood in front of the television, given a place of honor in order to view the brief, but thrilling footage, and watched. Stared. Relived.

The others were so busy looking at the screen, they didn't notice that the pulse beat at her throat quickened. Or that her hands started to shake.

Houston noticed, and the urge to fold his arms around her was so strong, his muscles strained to obey. But he didn't, of course. She would probably think he was crazy or overeager. Or both. Besides, he thought, noticing the tiny beads of perspiration along her upper lip, she was strung tight as a bowstring. If anyone touched her right now, she would probably jump out of her skin.

He leaned forward and whispered in her ear. "Pretty gutsy thing to do."

"I was too scared to move," she said without taking her eyes off the screen, as Lonnie rewound the tape to show it for the fourth or fifth time.

"Not in the water. Here."

Abby turned her head and looked into his eyes. He was a stranger, yet without a word from her, somehow he realized what it had cost her to watch the tape. To relive her fear. Not only did he realize, but he sympathized.

Despite her tight rein on her emotions, tears gathered in her eyes. "Can't . . . I—"

Before she could finish her sentence, Houston put his hands on her shoulders and turned her toward him. "We're getting out of here." He grabbed her hand and pulled her out of the shop and into the sunshine.

"Where are we going?" she finally asked, after obediently following along for almost half a block.

"You need food."

"I'm not hungry."

"Yes, you are."

"No."

"Well, you're going to eat anyway."

"I can't."

"Yes, you can."

"No!" She jerked her hand out of his. "What the hell do you think you're doing? I don't want food. And I damn sure don't want you telling me what to do."

He pulled her around a corner onto a side street. "What do you want, Abigail?"

Working up to a full head of steam, she completely missed the fact that he was on a first-name basis. "For you to get the hell away from me," she said through clenched teeth.

"No, you don't."

"Get—away."

"No." His response was flat. Definite.

And enraging.

The rage boiled up from the center of her soul like an erupting volcano. Abby slapped him. Hard. Then she slapped him again.

Houston never flinched, never retreated so much as an inch.

"Feel better?"

Stunned at her behavior, Abby simply nodded.

"Figured you would."

"I—I . . . hit you. I'm so sorry."

"But you *do* feel better."

Abby suddenly realized that she did feel better. A lot better. Thanks to Houston Sinclair. "You made me mad."

He grinned. Not a grin of satisfaction, but pleasure. "Finally. Had me worried for a minute. You didn't need food, you just needed to vent."

"You wanted me to slap you." She stated the obvious.

"And you let me have it." He stroked his stinging cheek. "In spades."

"So I would—"

"Snap out of it," he finished for her. "You were about to blow a fuse if some of that fear and anger didn't find a release valve."

"How did you know?"

The grin drooped slightly. "Experience."

"Well," Abby said, her voice shaky. "I don't know what to say."

"'Thank you' works."

"Thank you. Very much." She touched his cheek. "Did I hurt you?"

His groin tightened, and his body flashed hot, cold, then hotter. "No sweat," he replied, his words the exact opposite of what he was feeling.

Abby knew she should remove her hand, but she didn't. She also knew she should find some way to return this encounter—this contact—to a more impersonal level. But instead, she let the moment, and her hand against his cheek, linger.

She told herself this was all part of the plan. And for the most part, she believed it. "Let me make it up to you."

Houston decided his blood pressure might just go through the roof if he didn't put a stop to her touching him. To what he was thinking as she touched him. But instead, he touched her.

He lifted her hand and kissed her palm. "Not necessary, Abigail."

For the third time that day, Abby held her breath. But unlike her encounter with the shark, she wasn't afraid to move. In fact, she was stunned at how strong her desire was to move. Closer to him. Against him.

"But if you insist," Houston said, his breath warm on her skin, "we could go to dinner."

"We could." It *would* help the investigation. And she could handle an intimate dinner with this man. She could do that. Of course, she could.

"Number?"

"What number?"

"Of your condo."

"Oh, yes." She took her hand away. "Kaanapal—"

"Kaanapali Shores."

"Y-you have a good memory."

Unexpectedly, his dark eyes flashed even darker. "For some things."

When she still didn't give him the information, he said, "I'd like to add your room number to the list."

"Oh, y-yes. One thirty-six, and . . ."

"Yes?"

"Under the circumstances . . . Well, most people call me Abby."

"Seven o'clock sound okay to you, Abby?"

"Fine."

"See ya then."

As Abby watched Houston Sinclair walk away, the thought crossed her mind that if she wasn't careful, she could be letting herself in for more trouble than she had ever bargained for.

Chapter 4

"Any more word from Seattle P.D.?" Abby shifted the cellular phone from one ear to the other.

"Faxing info even as we speak," Brax said.

"And?" She glanced over at the portable fax machine sitting on the breakfast bar, six feet from the table where she had the case file and her notes spread out in front of her.

"Not much. You?"

"The same. But I did meet the boys today."

"And how did that go?"

She tucked the phone under her chin, walked over, and pulled out the fax. "I'm having dinner with Sinclair tonight."

"Good girl. Moving right along. What about Leland?"

Abby could almost hear Brax's long-distance smile. "He's on the agenda for tomorrow."

"Playing one against the other?"

"Not really. I don't think I'm Leland's type. I was in their dive shop today, and he never so much as gave me a tumble."

"Must be losing your grip."

"Gee, thanks. I'm just supposed to find out what makes the guy tick. Not crawl in bed with him."

When she didn't comment on Houston, he asked the obvious. "What about Sinclair?"

"He's...not what I expected," she replied, hoping her voice didn't betray any of her own fears concerning Houston.

"How so?"

"If he's a scam artist, he's sure got an offbeat technique." Provoking a woman into slapping your face was definitely not an approach she would put at the top of the list of smooth moves. Of course, she could confirm that offbeat or not, Houston Sinclair was most definitely charming. And incredibly handsome.

"Well, my money's on you, Miss Abigail."

"I just keep feeling there's something we've missed. Something right under our noses."

"You've read the EUOs," he said, referring to the examination-under-oath depositions required by law.

Abby had read Sinclair's and Leland's EUOs from top to bottom, front and back, inside out and still couldn't put her finger on the elusive clue her instincts were telling her was there. She had to look again.

She sighed. "Yeah. But I'll go over them again. In the meantime, how about having another arson expert take a look at the first expert's findings. Never hurts to get a second opinion."

"In a mood to spend company money, huh?"

"What's a few hundred dollars stacked up against a half million?"

"Point taken. Let me know when you come up with anything," Brax said, and hung up.

"When I come up with anything. *If* I come up with anything," Abby muttered.

She picked up the copy of Gil Leland's examination-under-oath, and started to read. Ten minutes later she put it down. A big fat zero. It was short and sweet. Gil Leland had been waiting in Hilo, Hawaii, for his partner to show up and finalize a contract with a mainland tour company. He'd had no idea his wife would be on board with his partner. And he had no idea why the boat exploded. He could only hazard a guess that something had malfunctioned.

Basically, he was clueless.

The accompanying information indicated that while Leland's personal finances were not exactly a fortune, he made a decent living. He had a respectable reputation in the business community, liked a good joke, and appeared to have no enemies.

Nothing there she could hang her hat on.

As far as background went, he came from a middle-class family, attended college on a scholarship, graduated in the top ten percent of the San Francisco Police Academy.

Routine. Maybe that's what bothered her. It felt too routine. Her instincts were seldom unreliable, but there was a first time for everything. Maybe she was just reaching because she had absolutely nothing to go on except the information from Seattle and Brax's hunch.

She tossed the form onto the table, and picked up Houston's EUO.

The interview had been conducted by an adjuster, with a lawyer from the corporate office present. Houston had been accompanied by his own lawyer. The questions were asked, and answered, she could add, in a straightforward manner. Everything had been done by the book. After dispensing with the obligatory identification, verification-of-residency, time-and-date ques-

tions, the interviewer, a Mr. Daly, asked Houston to
recount, to the best of his knowledge, the events of the
day of the accident, beginning when the *Two of a Kind*
left Lahaina Harbor.

Abby had, of course, read the EUO before, evaluat-
ing its content as she would any other case. They were
just words on paper, transcribed word for word. But
this time, as she read them, she visualized Houston's
face. As she did, she found herself visualizing his pain.

Daly: And you say you repeatedly called out to
Mrs. Leland?

Sinclair: Yes.

Daly: How long before she responded?

Sinclair: I don't know. Seemed like hours. Probably only seconds. You see, the fire was roaring.
And it just seemed to—to devour the boat.

Daly: Making it impossible to get to her.

Sinclair: No. Yes. I thought. That is, I had to try.
I just kept telling her to hang on. I said, "Hang on,
Shel. I'm coming." And I tried.

Daly: You say you were finally able to climb back
on board?

Sinclair: Yes. Tried to grab for the wheel. I knew
if I could pull myself up to the left hull, I could get
to her, but . . .

Daly: That's when the second explosion knocked
you back into the water?

Sinclair: Yes.

Daly: And you actually saw the boat sink?

Sinclair: Yes. Yes.

Daly: Afterward, did you see any debris, or Mrs.
Leland's body?

Sinclair: Yes, and—and no. I saw the ship's bell.
Or what was left of it.

Daly: The bell was floating?

Sinclair: No. It was still bolted to a piece of the hull.

Daly: How large a piece?

Sinclair: Small. Maybe one by two feet.

Daly: You say a bell was attached to it?

Sinclair: Yes. Standard brass bell. Most ships have them. It was engraved with the ship's name and the date we went into business.

Daly: Did you consider picking up the piece of fiberglass, and putting it in the raft with you?

Sinclair: What?

Daly: Did you consider picking up—

Sinclair: You want to know why I didn't think about collecting debris when I had just seen someone I cared about die?

Daly: I merely—

Sinclair: No. I didn't pick up the damn bell. How the hell can you even ask such a question? Do you know what horror is, Mr. Daly?

Daly: I'm sorry if I—

Sinclair: Real horror? Well, I do. And you know what it is? It's helplessness. It's knowing that if you had been just a second quicker—

Daly: Sit down, Mr. Sinclair.

Sinclair: Your best friend's wife would be laughing in the sun right now instead of lying at the bottom of the goddamn Pacific!

Abby read the entire EUO, but that particular block of questions and answers had stuck with her. Haunted her, actually, because for a few moments she had felt Houston's anguish.

Understandable, but it was also a red flag telling her to back away, retain her objectivity.

An investigator was only supposed to be concerned with getting the answers to four basic questions.

Cause.

Opportunity for cause.

Origin of fire.

Motive.

Without any physical evidence Abby couldn't determine cause, opportunity for cause, or origin of fire. That left her with motive. And so far, she had come up empty-handed on that one, as well.

Maybe this evening would provide her with a chance to get more information. Maybe tonight she could find out who Houston Sinclair really was.

She was late. Lingering over Houston's EUO had been as interesting as the first time she'd read it. And as time-consuming, only more so. The first time, she'd never met him or even wanted to. Now, she had not only met him, but she was beginning to feel as if she knew him. And that was dangerous. As dangerous as the intimate moment they had shared. She had slapped his cheek, and he had kissed her palm.

Abby glanced at her hand and, noticing her watch, was shocked to see the hour. One hurried shower and frantic makeup session later, she was still running behind.

Dinner. He'd said dinner. But where? And what did she wear?

Sundress. A sundress and sandals. She was in the Hawaiian Islands, for goodness' sake. How far wrong could she go in a dressy linen sundress and strappy low-heeled sandals? Besides, it wasn't like this was a *date* date. Everything she did was to enhance her cover story in order to find out more about Leland and Sinclair. So, what was she fussing about?

Abby looked in the mirror, unsatisfied with her appearance. The humidity had turned her natural waves into a riot of curls.

"Great," she muttered to her reflection. "You look like Little Orphan Annie." She glanced at her watch. "And you're late, Annie."

He was early. Even knowing his timing was a sign of overeagerness, Houston had sped down Honoapi'ilani Highway like a high-school nerd headed for his first and only date. He had to remind himself no less than three times to ease back on the accelerator of Gil's Jeep. He would have preferred to pick her up in his classic T-Bird, but it was in the shop.

His eagerness surprised him. But no less than the realization that he wanted to impress her. When was the last time he had looked forward to spending time with a beautiful woman?

Before the accident. Before he had lost his courage.

And if Houston were truthful, even before that. After Gil and Shelley married, things had changed. He had changed. Although he was long past the need to prove his virility, he still went out a couple of times a week, but none of the women left any lasting impressions. The ladies, and the good times, seemed to blend into a homogenized memory. Indistinctive and forgettable.

Words that certainly didn't apply to Abigail Douglass.

Abigail. Prim and proper. The name made him think of filmy summer dresses ruffled by a breeze, and wide-brimmed hats with flowers banded around the crown.

Abby. Soft and alluring. The name made him think of hot summer nights and slow, wet kisses.

Two sides to the same woman.

Interesting. And getting more so by the minute, Houston decided as he pulled into the entrance of the Kaanapali Shores Hotel and condos, parked Gil's Jeep, and walked through the breezeway lobby.

He knocked on the door twice before she answered.

"Aloha," he said.

She was flushed, her cheeks slightly damp, but prettily so. And her feet were bare. Which meant either she felt comfortable enough with herself and him not to bother, or she was running late.

Yes, definitely the most interesting woman Houston had met in a long time. A very long time.

"Alo— Hi. Come on in. I'm running a bit late."

Houston grinned. Oh, well, they would get to "comfortable" sooner or later. Sooner if he had his way.

"Too much shopping?"

"Uh, yes. I, uh, guess I just lost track of time." She had made scrupulously certain there were no traces of notes or files left lying about. She didn't want him asking questions about why a tourist would bring her work along on vacation.

"You buy that today?" He indicated the caramel-colored dress that set off her strawberry-blond hair.

"No. I brought it from home. Like it? It has a jacket, but I decided against it tonight."

He liked the dress and what was in it. "Perfect."

She sighed as if relieved. "I'll just be a minute," she said, and disappeared into a bedroom.

"Where's home?" he asked after a minute or two.

She walked back into the room wearing sandals. "California. How about you?"

"Galveston, Texas, ma'am." He tipped an imaginary Stetson. "Ever been there?"

"Don't think so," she lied. She had once spent three days there working on a case.

"Bet you'd like it. Lots of charm."

"Sounds..." She looked up and straight into his dark brown eyes. "Charming."

He stepped closer. "You look delicious." Reaching out, he brushed a wisp of strawberry-blond curl away from her damp cheek.

Abby found the gesture, and his choice of words, strangely intimate. And unnerving. But she refused to allow him to sidetrack her as he had that morning. She grinned. "You must be hungry."

"Starved." Houston heard himself speak the word, and realized the statement applied to more than food. Abby was a feast for the eyes, all right. But it was more. A hunger he hadn't even known existed, demanded satisfaction. A hunger for something soft and alluring. Prim and proper. Something substantial.

She liked the way he was looking at her. And she didn't. Unless she was mistaken, the way he was looking at her would make her job a lot easier. But there was something about the look in his eyes that told her *easy* was not the optimum word here. *Desire* would have been more accurate. The word *desire,* coupled with *predatory.*

He wanted her. She saw it clearly in the way he looked at her. In the seductive tone of his voice. Even in his body language. No beating around the bush. Just plain, old-fashioned, basic desire.

"Wh-where are we going?"

The doubled-edged question almost struck her as funny, except for the fact that he was so close she could feel his body heat. If she wasn't careful, this could take them places neither of them was prepared to go.

"Not far."

Abby nodded. "I'll get my purse." And a little distance, she thought.

As it turned out, they didn't have far to go. Only down a walkway lined with banana trees and plumeria bushes, and around a corner to the hotel's cabana-style restaurant. The dining areas were small, candlelit and facing the ocean. Perfect for viewing breathtaking sunsets.

"Why is it," Abby asked, gazing at the blazing orange, red and gold sky as she sipped her Kahlúa-laced coffee, "you have to come thousands of miles to really appreciate sunsets? I know the same sunsets in California, but it sure looks different here."

"It is different. Because of the water. It's like watching fire dance across a mirror." As soon as the words formed on his lips, memories popped through his mind like flashbulbs, illuminating fragments without offering any real clarity. When it happened, and it was happening more often of late, he still fought to shut out the pain he knew the memories would bring. But there was a part of him—infinitesimal though it might be—that whispered remembering might bring hope. The hope that he could finally put his torment to rest.

Houston looked away from the dazzling spectacle of nature and focused on his own coffee.

"How was your *mahimahi*? he asked, referring to the local catch of the day.

"Fantastic." Obviously, his comment about fire on a mirror had reminded him of the accident. And just as obviously, he had shut the memory down. Fast. Somehow she had to get him to open up and talk to her about what had happened. And from what she had seen so far, she had her work cut out for her.

"How about a sunset walk on the beach?" he suggested as the waiter cleared away the remnants of their meal. "It's mandatory, your first day in paradise."

"Really? Well, then, lead on. I wouldn't want the paradise police after me."

As they headed toward the beach, Abby cast a sideways glance at her escort, and was impressed all over again with his good looks. He was a devilishly handsome man, no question about it. Tall, well-built, with a loose-legged stride that was both cocky and confident at the same time. And the kind of male charisma that women simply couldn't ignore, no matter if it was one-on-one or in a crowded room. Abby could state, unequivocally, that one-on-one was an unbelievably intense experience.

"Have you booked another dive for tomorrow?"

"No," she answered a little too quickly, too adamantly.

"What about a whale watch? Or snorkeling?"

"I'm not sure yet." She didn't have the nerve to tell him that the idea of getting back on the water, much less getting *in* it, was still upsetting. "What do you do for fun?"

Fun? He hardly knew how to answer her. It seemed like years since he had even entertained the prospect of real fun. He and Gil had flown to Honolulu on a couple of occasions and tried to recapture something of the good old days. The lights were as bright, and the ladies were as soft. But for Houston, it was no good.

"Fun hasn't been a big part of my agenda lately."

"Oh," was all she said, leaving the door open for him. Hopefully, to talk about the accident.

He said nothing for several minutes. Finally they reached a wrought-iron gate that led down to the beach. He bent over, untied the laces on one of his deck shoes and took it off. "Take off your shoes," he suggested, removing his other shoe.

"Hmm?"

"The sand."

"Oh, yes."

Without thinking, she put her hand on his shoulder to balance herself as she leaned over to undo first one sandal, then the other. Holding both shoes in one hand, sole to sole, she straightened. After removing the additional two inches, Abby discovered she was now just the right height to put her head on his shoulder. If she chose to put her head on his shoulder. Which, of course, she didn't. Couldn't. Keep it light, she told herself.

"Maybe we can change your agenda," she suggested.

He liked the way the humidity made her hair curl wildly around her face. And the way the sunset turned those strawberry-blond curls into glorious red gold. "What for?"

"So you can start having some fun."

"I can start right now." He put his hand on her waist, and ever so gently urged her closer.

"Good." Things were moving faster than she had planned. *He* was moving faster than she had expected. She should have resisted when he pulled her even closer. But she didn't.

"I think so." Houston dipped his head, and kissed her.

He tested her mouth for softness, sweetness; slowly, gently at first, then deeper, coaxing her lips to part. Behind him, the surf crashed against the shoreline in age-old rhythms as the tide rose. Rhythms he longed to replicate. Body to body. His to hers.

Abby kissed him back. Sort of. She stopped just short of leaning into the kiss. His mouth was warm, and his mustache brushed her lips like a master painter stroking an all-too-willing canvas. This was all part of her cover, she told herself. All part of a job. But his kiss was driving all thoughts of work out of her mind.

He tasted slightly of Kahlúa, and she was shocked at how much she wanted to take the kiss further. How much she wanted to press herself against him. To feel him against her. But she didn't. She wasn't immune to a little romance, but she knew where to draw the line. The line was here. Now.

Despite all of that, she let her mouth linger on his for a second longer than it should have.

When he lifted his head, she looked into his eyes. "I was never much good at summer romances," she told him in a very Abigail tone of voice.

"It's spring." Despite the fact that she had kissed him back, he read mistrust in her soft blue eyes.

"You know what I'm talking about."

"Let's see." With both his hands now at her waist, he glanced heavenward as if the words he wanted were written across the stars. "To begin with, you're not that kind of girl. Definitely not interested in a vacation fling. Or a quick roll in the hay—uh, sand. In a week or so... you want to be home enjoying your snapshots... not regretting a few hormone-driven hot nights. That about cover it?"

"Just about. At least you understand where I'm coming from." Flippant. He was way too flippant to suit her taste. But then, what had she expected? He was, after all, who he was. A man who courted adventure, women and danger with the same savor-the-moment attitude. Why was it she had to keep reminding herself of that fact?

"I may understand, but that doesn't mean I'll give up."

"And that doesn't mean that I intend to end up as another notch on the handle of some man's ego."

"Nothing to do with ego. For the first time in a long time, I know what I want. And when you know what you want, why waste time playing games?"

"I thought the objective was fun." Abby knew she had slipped out of her role-playing. Bits and pieces of the real Abby were showing through and she forced herself to remember why she was doing this. It helped her regain control.

The breeze sent a strand of hair dancing across her cheek. He brushed it aside. "Don't know about you, but I'm having a ball."

"Well…" She stepped away from him, irritated with herself that the action had taken so much effort. "The ball is rolling a bit too fast for me."

"All right. But…" He grabbed her hand. "Be warned, Abigail. You're far too bright and beautiful to be left alone in paradise."

And he was far too smooth. She needed distance.

"Do you get a lot of women with this—" she waved her hand, pinkie and thumb only extended in the Hawaiian "Hang loose, don't worry" hand sign "—beachcomber approach of yours?"

"I haven't had any complaints."

"Undoubtedly. But I'm not what you're used to," she said truthfully.

"Presumptuous, aren't you?"

"I just meant—"

"You have no idea what I'm used to." He released her hand, and they resumed their walk.

There was an edge to his voice that hadn't been there a second ago.

Avoiding the surf, they walked along the shore toward an outcropping of lava rock that rose out of the sand like a humpback whale breaching. The last golden rays of the day hit the spray as waves broke over the rock's craggy surface, creating rainbows.

Abby called herself several kinds of idiot. That kind of slip of the tongue was strictly junior-grade stuff. What was she thinking? Maybe she really was losing her touch.

"I'm sorry," she said, at last. "You're right. I have no idea what kind of woman you're used to dating. It's just that you're good-looking, successful and charming. And I assumed you would be interested in the same kind of woman."

"What are you? Chopped liver?"

"No." She smiled. "I just meant—"

"Tell you what, Miss Abigail—"

She stopped walking. "Why did you call me that?"

"Because it suits you when you're being very prim and proper. The way you are now."

"Oh."

"Let's say you and I agree not to deal in generalities. I'll refrain from making any misleading assumptions about you. And you do the same about me."

"Misleading? You think I've misled you?" Was it possible he could know who she was? Why she was here?

"I think you're a beautiful woman. Warm, gentle. And I think finding out who you are is going to be one sweet adventure."

"You may be disappointed."

"Why?"

She shrugged. "This is it. Plain and simple. No deep dark secrets. No hidden agenda," she lied. "I'm just what I appear to be."

"No one," he said, "is just what they appear to be. And everyone has dark secrets. Some darker than others."

Chapter 5

Abby couldn't get Houston's comment that some secrets were darker than others, out of her mind. It had been her last conscious thought before dropping off to sleep. And practically her first thought this morning.

As she made her way into Lahaina behind the wheel of her rented sedan, she wondered just how dark his secrets were. Dark enough to include extortion and fraud? From her professional point of view, if push came to shove, the number of people who had that kind of larceny in their hearts would produce shocking figures on any newscast.

But what motive would Houston have? What did he stand to gain by blowing his own boat out of the water?

The catamaran had been replaced by a less expensive, but perfectly seaworthy boat. Certainly not condemning in itself. After suffering such a loss, quite often people were leery of sinking a big chunk of money into replacement items. That included everything from video cameras to million-dollar residences. That didn't necessarily indicate fraud.

In fact, none of the information at her disposal pointed to criminal activity, but that didn't do anything to mollify her instincts to the contrary. Predictably, insurance companies looked at policyholders first. They were the logical suspects. And even though she didn't discount it, in this case she had a feeling there was more to it.

Still, the unanswered question of what became of the remaining funds nagged at her investigator's mind. If the money had been poured back into Lone Star Dive Shop & Tours, it would be evident. Maybe not on a large scale, but there would be evidence. All she had to do was find it.

Abby wheeled the sedan into a parking space across the street from the dive shop. She turned off the motor, but didn't get out. On the drive in from her condo all her thoughts had been focused on business.

Now, she could no longer avoid the other thoughts. The strictly personal ones that she had deliberately shoved to the back of her mind. Would have shoved *out* of it, if she could have. Thoughts of Houston's handsome face. Of his up-front attitude regarding what he wanted. Namely, her.

And then there was his kiss.

Oh, yes. His kiss.

Although, to be brutally honest, she couldn't claim it was only his kiss. After all, she had kissed him back. But with a purpose, of course.

A purpose, she reminded herself, that was the reason she was here in the first place. So he was a great kisser. So what? So for just a moment, just a split second, she had felt the familiar and oh-so-longed-for warmth. So what? She was human. Human or not, she just couldn't allow it to happen again.

Resolve. Determination. That's what was called for, here.

Abby got out of the car, and stood tall. She was resolved and determined not to allow Houston Sinclair or his smooth charm to sidetrack her from her responsibilities.

As she started across the street, she noticed a classic 1957 powder blue Thunderbird convertible parked in front of the dive shop. The car was in perfect condition, and an absolute knockout. As a teenager, a T-Bird was her fantasy car, and an up-close look at one this pristine was a treat. She admired the car for several minutes, then went into the shop.

But when she walked in the door and saw Houston talking to Gil, standing there all bronzed and gorgeous, the resolve and determination she had thought so strong only moments earlier, wavered ever so slightly. And she wondered why the "real" woman's heart she wasn't supposed to have was beating so fast.

He was wearing swim trunks, sandals, a tan and a smile. Nothing else. Her stomach did a somersault. Two, in fact.

"Hi."

"Hi, yourself." He shook his head. "I was wrong."

Abby blinked. About the kiss? Was he about to apologize for doing what he did best—charming her? "About what?"

"Moonlight and sunsets do great things for a woman's complexion. I had almost convinced myself you couldn't possibly look as good as I remembered. Brother, was I wrong."

Reaching out, he stroked his knuckles along her cheek as if to verify his own conclusion. "You look better."

No one this charming—this disarmingly charming—could be sincere, she reminded herself. The reminder didn't slow her heart rate one bit. "Thanks."

When he dropped his hand she hated herself for feeling disappointed. Hated having to clench her own hands into fists to keep from reaching for his; to keep from pulling it back to her cheek. Her nails bit half-moon-shaped marks into her palms.

"What's on your agenda?"

"Agenda? Oh, not much."

"Decide to book another dive?"

"No. No dives today."

"Whale watch?"

She shrugged. "Maybe." It was a lie she hoped wasn't reflected in her eyes or voice. No whale watches today or any day. Not unless she could watch them from the shore.

"We've probably got a spot or two left. Check with Stuart to see how booked up we are."

"Oh, no, that's all right."

"I'd do it for you, but I'm on my way out."

"Taking out a group to dive?"

"No." The denial was flat and a little cold. Once again, she had the feeling that there was something he didn't want her to know.

He must have realized how cold he sounded, because he smiled and said, "Don't spread this around, but Gil is a much better dive master than I am."

"Who?" she asked, pretending not to know who he was talking about.

"Gil Leland, my partner."

"Heard that, slick." A grinning Gil walked up behind Houston. "And you're right."

"Gil," Houston said. "Have you met Ms. Douglass?"

"Not formally. But anyone that can swim with the sharks is aces in my book. Abby, isn't it?" He shook her hand. "How'ya doing?"

"Great." Unless she counted the sudden dryness in her throat, and the trembling in her hands. The mere mention of the shark was enough to make her heart beat faster.

"You sure are," Gil agreed. "Great for business. I'll bet you a hundred dollars we've had no less than ten calls today wanting to book dives."

Abby opened her mouth to respond, but before she could, Houston spoke up. "Don't bet with him."

"Oh, here we go." Gil rolled his eyes.

"Somebody needs to warn her that anytime you use the phrase, 'I'll bet you,' she should run for the hills. This man will bet on anything."

"Don't listen to him," Gil told her. "He's just jealous because he has such lousy luck. However—" his gaze swept Abby up and down "—I have to say his luck is improving."

"Back off," Houston ordered.

"Ouch." Gil released Abby's hand, and shook his own as if in response to an imaginary burn. "You must be one hot number."

Houston lifted an eyebrow. "Too hot for you."

"Oh. Like that, is it?"

"Like that."

"Excuse me," Abby interjected.

Both men's gazes turned to her.

"You two were so busy being macho, I thought you might have forgotten I was here." She was smiling, but neither of them was stupid enough to accept the smile at face value.

"Sorry." Gil grinned.

Leland had the kind of cocky, little-boy grin so many women found irresistible. Abby didn't find it one bit irresistible. In fact, it grated on her nerves. Of course, she refused to allow her irritation to show. Instead, she would play whatever games were necessary. It was, after all, part of her plan.

"So am I," Houston said, sincerely. "Can I make it up to you tonight?"

"I don't know. Maybe I should make you suffer." Her intent had been to keep the exchange light, flirtatious. But when she looked into Houston's eyes, she realized she wasn't flirting. A secret part of her did want to make him suffer. Not because of any show of blatant chauvinistic behavior, but because he had caused her to grapple for control last night.

"You will if you turn me down."

She wanted to. For just a second, she wanted to turn around and walk straight out of Houston Sinclair's life. Or, more truthfully, she wanted him out of hers. Neither would work. This was her job, and she had to do it. "How could I, after such a charming comment?"

"I was counting on that."

He leaned close to her. "Seven still good for you?"

His face was so close to hers, she could almost count his eyelashes. Close enough to slap. Or kiss. Abby simply answered, "Yes."

"Dress casual. We're eating in the open air."

"Shorts okay?"

Houston grinned. "I wouldn't be the least bit heartbroken to spend an evening admiring those long, gorgeous legs of yours." Before she realized his intent, he leaned over and kissed her lightly, quickly on the mouth.

Then he walked to the door, opened it, and glanced back. "And watch out for sharks." He pointed at Gil. "Especially the two-legged ones." And then he disappeared out the door.

Gazing at him through the window, Abby couldn't keep herself from grinning. She tried, but it didn't work. Houston Sinclair was too charming for her own good. And to top it off, he climbed into her dream car and drove away.

"Great guy."

She turned around. "Looks like it." She had almost forgotten Gil Leland was still standing there.

"Oh, he is. Take my word."

Here was her chance to probe Leland's personality. And, under the guise of wanting to know all she could about a man she was interested in, ask questions about Houston at the same time. The opportunity was far too good to pass up.

"I take it you and Houston have known each other a long time."

He shrugged. "Just since the second grade."

"Whoa. If I had gone looking for a source of information, I couldn't have done a better job. You must know everything about him, from junior-high Halloween pranks that backfired to the number of girls he sneaked into his college dorm."

"Baby, you don't know the half of it. And since I was right beside him with my own sneaky treat, I can verify everything." He motioned to a small table set up with a coffee urn. "Buy you a cup?"

"Thanks," Abby said, and followed him.

The name "baby" grated on her nerves as much as his cocky grin, but she wasn't about to miss her golden opportunity.

He poured coffee for both of them. "Where would you like for me to start? Cream?"

"Black, please."

He handed her the cup. "I would just love to help you land old Houston."

"Who said anything about landing Houston?"

"You're obviously interested."

"I am. But don't book the church and order flowers. And please—" she held up her hands "—don't drag out the family photo albums. Your friend is terrific, but that's not where this is headed."

Gil shook his head. "Too bad. About time he latched on to a woman who didn't let that handsome face of his get in the way."

"What's that supposed to mean?"

He sipped his coffee. "Just that sometimes what's on the surface can be so attractive, no one bothers to look deeper."

"Maybe Houston wants it that way."

"To hear him tell it."

"But you don't agree?"

"Not for a minute." He took a long drink. "It's a cover."

"For what?"

"Pain."

Abby hadn't expected Leland to be so honest or so revealing. She pressed her luck. "Would I be insensitive if I asked, about what? Or who?"

Gil Leland stared into his now almost-empty coffee cup. "It's not my story to tell. Not really." Then he looked at Abby, and she saw genuine concern in his green eyes. "But he should talk about it to somebody, that's for sure."

"You think he's keeping something locked up inside himself. Something . . . painful."

"Yeah. And you can add 'mysterious.' Like the disappearing act he pulled a few minutes ago."

"You mean today? Just now?"

"Every day. Well, every other day, at least. He just goes off for a couple of hours. Nobody knows where. When I asked him, he told me to leave it alone." Gil shrugged. "See what I mean? Mysterious."

"It does sound...strange," Abby agreed. Where could Houston be going on these little jaunts? Her investigator's mind latched on to the tidbit of information like a snapping turtle. Did he meet someone? And for what purpose?

"Ah, hell. Guess a man's entitled to some down time. God knows, Houston's paid for his. Still—" Gil sighed "—the right woman could make a helluva lotta difference in his life. Shelley sure made a difference in mine."

"Shelley?"

"My wife." He looked away for a moment. "At least, she was."

"Divorce?" she asked, hoping she sounded sincere.

"No. She was killed in an accident. Nine months and ten days ago."

"I'm sorry."

Abby had to admit that she was surprised at the grief still so evident in his voice. Not to mention the way he had kept track of the time since his wife's death. Of course, she was looking at the situation from the point of view of his possible guilt. She still had no proof that Gil had anything to do with the explosion. And to be fair, the man had lost his wife. Loss, no matter what the circumstances, was painful.

"Thanks." This time when he smiled, the cockiness was gone. "She was terrific. All sassy and gorgeous. And she knew how to have fun. Not crazy, silly stuff, but, you know, really have fun. No matter where she was. She just loved life. And me."

After a pause he added, "That's what I want for Houston. I love to rib him about the fact that he let a good woman slip right through his fingers."

"I don't understand."

"He dated Shelley before I did. In fact, he introduced us. Ironic, huh?"

"Yes. That didn't bother you?"

"Why should it? She married me. Only time I can remember that I won and Houston lost, when it came to a woman." He looked away for a moment. "In the end we both lost. I'm just grateful I didn't lose both of my partners in that explosion."

"Explosion?"

"The accident that killed my wife. She and Houston were on board the company boat, headed for the big island. He survived. She...d-didn't," he said, his voice almost breaking.

Either this man was a consummate liar, or he was hurting for real. At the moment, Abby would have been hard-pressed to decide which. "I . . . I'm really sorry."

"Thanks. Houston took it almost as hard as I did. We just kinda help each other, and every day it gets a little easier."

"That kind of friendship is hard to find."

"You're telling me."

"At least you have that. And," she said, glancing around the shop, "you seem to have a thriving business."

"Yeah. We're doing okay in that department. Struggling, but okay. A new coat of paint on the outside wouldn't hurt, and maybe one of those new computerized cash registers, but like I said, we're doing okay."

"It's nice that there're two of you, so neither has to be tied to the shop full-time."

"We've always divided things up just about fifty-fifty. Or at least we did before the accident."

"But not now?" Abby knew she was pushing her luck, but she wanted more information. Anything that would give her another clue, point her in the right direction.

"Since the accident, Stuart and I do all the dives and whale watches. Houston takes care of the shop."

"He doesn't dive at all?"

"Nope."

"Not even for pleasure?"

Gil shook his head. And when Abby started to ask why, she knew she had pushed her luck as far as she could.

"Like I told you, it's not my story to tell. More coffee? Or am I keeping you from buying out all the stores on Front Street?" he asked, obviously changing the subject.

"Thanks. One cup's my limit."

"Smart lady. Sure I can't change your mind?"

"About what?"

"Getting seriously interested in my partner."

Abby smiled. "I'm a mainlander, remember? I'll be going home in a week or so."

"A lot can happen in a week."

A lot had *better* happen in a week, Abby thought as she left the dive shop a few minutes later. Her investigation was definitely sagging.

She was still thinking about the investigation when she pulled up to the red light at Papalaua, preparing to turn left onto Highway 30, heading to her condo. Suddenly she caught a glimpse of a blue Thunderbird convertible with a man driving as it zoomed through the green light.

On an impulse, and thankfully with an empty lane beside her, Abby whipped her rented sedan over into the far right lane, and turned to follow the T-Bird.

She stayed just close enough to keep the car in sight, and far enough back not to lose him.

It was Houston at the wheel. No mistake.

She followed him south into one of the residential districts, maintaining a cautious distance. But as it turned out, she was too cautious. He turned a corner, and when she caught up, his car was nowhere to be seen. She drove on for a couple of blocks, checking side streets, but came up empty-handed. Finally she went back to the corner where he had disappeared, in hopes that she could figure out what had happened.

Had he gone into one of the surrounding private residences? If so, where was his car? Inside the garage? It was possible, of course, that one of these houses could be his home.

She checked the address she had for Houston against the detailed map of Maui, and discarded that theory. So where was he?

Maybe it was a girlfriend's house.

Abby told herself the idea that Houston might have a lady friend didn't bother her. After all, he was a healthy, red-blooded male. She couldn't very well expect the man to live like a monk, could she?

Of course not. It was just that, well . . .

Well, dammit, Abby fumed. It was just that the idea of him romancing someone else at the same time he was cozying up to her was enough to make any woman mad. After the way he had kissed her, held her, *charmed* her . . .

Abby sighed, propping her elbows on the steering wheel. That damned word again. For a heartbeat she had acted as if he had gotten to her. Which, of course, was miles from the truth.

He hadn't gotten to her, because she wouldn't allow it. She certainly had no intention of making the same mistake twice. It didn't matter if he was charming. Or handsome. Or tender. It didn't matter that he made her feel . . . special. That he simply made her *feel*. It didn't matter.

But it was beginning to matter. A lot.

Everything about him was beginning to matter. That was why the thought of him seeing another woman had upset her. Even now, she was having trouble detaching her thoughts, concentrating on the case.

Okay, she thought, pulling herself back to the problem at hand. If Houston had a...a friend in this neighborhood, tracking the lady down might take time, but it could be done.

She glanced around. The only othe﹒ possibility in sight was a large two-story building adjacent to two soccer fields and a swimming pool. Abby drove by the front of the building and discovered it was a local recreation center.

Could this be the site of the mysterious disappearances Gil had mentioned? What on earth could Houston be doing in a rec center?

She waited and watched for another fifteen minutes without any results. Finally, she decided she had seen enough...of nothing.

Time to get specific with this investigation, Abby decided, an hour later back in her condo. That meant fine-tooth combing the file again. And maybe again. She was convinced there was something that she, Brax and the first investigator had missed. Something that would give her a leg up on proving whether or not the explosion was accidental or deliberate. Something that would reveal not only the cause, but possibly the culprit, as well.

Hours later, after having gone over the file again, literally from front to back, back to front, she resorted to her own unique detection process—one that had never failed to produce results.

She took a pen and legal-size notepad out of her briefcase, and began her show-and-tell system: a self-designed, organized layout to ''show'' where the missing pieces of her puzzle existed, and to ''tell'' her what questions she needed to ask in order to find the missing pieces.

Using her own brand of shorthand, on one side of the page she listed the events in sequence, and time frames. On the other side of the page she listed pertinent unanswered, or previously unasked, questions. When all of that was done, she wrote down the names of all of her suspects.

And what she had left was more holes than not. More questions than answers.

What she didn't have was a motive.

That is, if she discounted the niggling little question that had been at the back of her mind ever since her conversation with Gil Leland. Ever since she had learned that Shelley Leland had once been Houston Sinclair's girl.

Was it possible this entire case revolved around two men wanting the same woman? Was it possible that Shelley Leland was the reason for the explosion?

Gil had mentioned that Houston had dated Shelley, even introduced her to Gil. Did she dump him for Gil? Had Houston been forced to stand by, day after day, and watch the woman he loved, love another man? And had he then become so desperate that he killed her?

But that didn't make sense. Why hadn't he killed Leland? Then Shelley would have turned to him for comfort, and he would have had what he wanted. Of course, people had been known to snap, and kill the thing they loved.

Elbows propped on the table, Abby took a deep breath and slowly blew it out. She rested her chin in her hands. It didn't fit. It just didn't fit. When she was around Houston and Gil at the same time, she felt no undercurrents of hostility. She saw no indication of any hidden agenda. They didn't look, sound or act as if they were anything but friends. Good friends. If they were pretending, it was the acting job of the century.

She frowned, suddenly compelled to review Houston's EUO. Something nagged at her memory. Maybe the answer to one of her questions. She flipped through the file until she found the section she wanted.

According to the EUO, Houston testified that he had intended to sail the *Two of a Kind* alone that day. Shelley had decided to come along at the last minute.

"Well, that's that," she said out loud, letting the pages fall back into place.

There was always the possibility that Houston could have lied. But Abby didn't think so. Of course, therein lay the problem. Her instincts were telling her that Houston was innocent. But she had no proof.

And the last time she had relied on her instincts, she'd been dead wrong.

Except this time felt different. Was that a rationalization, she wondered? Another way to dress up the same mistake? It didn't feel that way, but admittedly, she wasn't the best judge of her emotional balance. Weren't her feelings for Houston proof of that? She was walking a fine line between professional expertise and personal involvement.

Unable to come down on one side or the other of the Houston guilty-or-not debate, she switched gears, focusing her thoughts on Gil. But she didn't have any more success trying to figure out his motive than she'd had with Houston.

Why would Gil Leland want his wife dead? He hadn't even known she was on board the catamaran. Houston was the only person who'd known.

Eyes closed, Abby massaged her temples. It always came back to Houston. "Right back where I started."

Her eyes snapped open. Houston wasn't the only person who had known Shelley was on the boat. Stuart Baker had known and probably the part-time native divers. But what reason would Baker have had to want his boss's wife dead? Or the part-timers, for that matter?

Maybe Shelley Leland had been having an affair with Stuart. She broke it off. He snapped and killed her.

Get a grip, Abby, she told herself. According to the file, ole Shelley was true-blue. Practically the epitome of the loving wife.

Lord, but she was tired. And dizzy from her mental round-robin with the information.

Stuart Baker was a possibility, regardless of how long he had been with Lone Star Dive Shop & Tours, but again Abby's instincts pointed toward "innocent." To be honest, she wondered how much she was relying on instinct, and how much she was basing on the fact that he had been so kind to her yesterday. He could have ignored her and let her stew in her own fear, but he hadn't. Instead, he had very gently, and without condescension, not only recognized, but actually validated her fear. Then he had given her time to collect her dignity before facing what he surely must have known was awaiting her—namely, a kind of celebrity, albeit unwanted.

Does that sound like the kind of man who kills? she asked herself.

"Enough." She pushed the file away from her. "I need facts, not conjecture." And she knew right where to get the help she needed. She took out a preprinted fax sheet and addressed it to Brax. Her request was simple. She wanted a complete background check on Stuart Baker, stem to stern. She also wanted specific information on Gil Leland's career as a San Francisco police officer—the good, bad, and ugly. And just so Brax wouldn't think she was playing favorites in any way, she requested information on Houston's naval career, from student to jet jockey. She pulled out her portable fax machine, sent the message, and leaned back in her chair.

That should do it.

One way or another, she intended to get her hands on some solid evidence.

Chapter 6

Feeling confident that she had done all she could, at least until she heard back from Brax, Abby decided to try and untangle her mind from the case for an hour or two. Maybe it would improve her perspective. Her intention had been to catch some sun and tackle a novel she had been trying to wade through. And her intentions had been good. They just didn't hold up. Abby soon found all her thoughts again focused on Houston.

She had to step up her contact with him. Get closer to him. The more he trusted her, the more likely he was to talk to her about the explosion. So, she would work harder to win his trust. After all, it was her job. And she was good at it.

Insurance-claim investigation wasn't for anyone who required constant support or affirmation. Usually it meant dealing with individuals who were willing to commit fraud, mayhem, even murder for money. Usually it meant delving into people's personal and profes-

sional lives in a very thorough and—yes—intimate way.
And it almost always meant dealing with those individuals, their lives and possible misdeeds, alone.

Oh, sure, Abby knew she had the full and considerable technical support system of the home office. And of course, people like Brax. All of which was well and good. But in the final analysis it was Abby, one-on-one with suspects. Abby tracking down information. Abby piecing together clues. Abby on her own, doing what she did best.

That was the way it was supposed to be. The way it had always been. The way it still should be.

But it wasn't. And hadn't been since she had taken this case. Since she had met Houston Sinclair.

Maybe she had lost her touch; was rusty from sitting behind a desk rather than out in the field.

No, she cautioned herself. That kind of thinking was negative, and detrimental to her and the investigation. Every case was different. Each one had its own idiosyncrasies and patterns. And she had a real gift for picking up those patterns and peculiarities. That gift, combined with a detail-oriented mind and a relentless curiosity, made her an ace investigator.

She was good at what she did. One of the best. Hadn't Brax said so often enough? Hadn't she worked hard to justify his opinion? As a matter of fact, she had worked damn hard to get where she was. For one reason only: not just to be the best, but to have done it without the help of a man—any man.

And she had. She had done what her mother had never been able to do—stand on her own two feet, be her own person.

Abby was proud of everything she had accomplished. She had succeeded where her mother had failed. Almost.

Riley had been a step backward. A slipup. But one she wouldn't make again, because she had learned from her mistake. Part of the reason Riley happened in the first place was because she had so little experience when it came to men. Could she help it if her abilities and ambition had precluded relationships? She had prioritized her life before she graduated from college, deciding that marriage and children were way down on the list.

In hindsight, she could see that she had been ripe for the picking when Riley happened along. Underneath all her ambition, all her drive and intelligence, was a basic loneliness that had never been appeased; an emptiness deep in her soul that she had never been able to fill. And Riley had seen her loneliness, and used it. Lord, but he was so charming she hadn't even realized what he was doing until it was almost too late.

Now, here she was, facing another charm boy. Only this time was different. She was older, and definitely wiser. She knew how to avoid the pitfalls.

So, why did she find herself thinking about Houston more often, not less? Why did she feel she had to include him in her request for updated information in order to exclude any notions of favoritism? Why did she find herself giving him the benefit of a doubt more so than her other suspects?

And why, she wondered, was the idea of having dinner with him so nerve-racking that she had spent the last ten minutes trying to justify who and what she was? Trying to convince herself that she could handle anything Houston Sinclair might throw her way.

Dressed in teal-colored linen shorts and a matching sleeveless blouse, Abby stopped when she caught a glimpse of herself in the full-length mirror hanging on the back of the bathroom door. She stepped closer, peering into the reflection of her own eyes.

Was that what all her mental hand-wringing had been about? A bad case of sagging self-confidence?

Of course it was, she hurriedly assured herself. She just needed to get back in the saddle, so to speak, after being behind a desk for so long. Things were clicking along. By tomorrow or the next day, she would have some, if not all, of the information she wanted. Everything would start to fall into place.

Abby took a deep breath. Yeah, she would be fine. She could handle anything that came along. Including an intimate dinner. Another moonlight stroll. Even another—there was a knock on the door—kiss?

She took several more deep breaths, went to the door and opened it. And was stunned all over again at how handsome he was.

He smiled, and those gorgeous velvet brown eyes of his swept down, and back up. "You look great."

She was so far past great, she had stepped right over to delicious, luscious, tempting. So tempting, in fact, that he wanted to step inside, lock the door, strip her bare, and kiss every square inch of her body.

"Thanks. You said casual."

His gaze again swept down to her legs. "And I see you decided against breaking my heart." A heart, he could have added, that was beating hard. Beating, pulsing, along with some other very vital parts of his body.

"I'm ready whenever you are," she said, smiling at him.

"C'mon." He reached for her hand. "Before I take you up on that."

Abby had flipped the lock and closed the door behind her before she realized the implication in her words. And his. "I just meant—"

Houston laughed, the sound a soft, deep rumble in his chest. "Don't worry, Miss Abigail. I'm not planning on a night of debauchery." They took several steps before he added, "Yet."

In the parking lot he steered her toward the Thunderbird convertible.

"Wow," Abby said, as if seeing it for the first time. He helped her inside, and closed the door. "What's this, your babemobile?"

"This beauty," he assured her as he slid behind the wheel, "is my only vice." He gave her a three-fingered salute. "Scout's honor."

"You want me to believe you were a Boy Scout?"

He drove out of the parking lot and onto Honoapi'ilani Highway. "Made it all the way to Eagle. And I've got the certificate to back me up. Wanna see it?"

"Is that a new twist on 'Want to come up and see my etchings?'"

"I don't own any etchings. Got a couple of cheap prints and an illustrated diver's calendar, if that turns you on."

"No, thanks."

"I thought most women had a yen to get a look at a man's home so they could see if he's a slob or not. See if he's decent husband material or not."

"Oh, yeah. We live for that kind of stuff." She rolled her eyes. "You're living in the wrong decade, pal."

"Ah, a liberated woman."

"I prefer 'independent.'"

After a lengthy pause in the conversation, Abby said, "So, are you?"

He grinned. "Am I what?"

"A slob?"

He shrugged. "Semi."

"Typical."

"I thought we weren't going to deal in generalities."

"Sorry. I was making one of those misleading assumptions, wasn't I?"

"Guilty as charged."

His choice of words was a timely reminder that this evening was business, not pleasure. Particularly since Abby was beginning to enjoy herself far too much.

"You're not even the least bit curious about my bachelor's lair?"

"Asked the Big Bad Wolf of Little Red Riding Hood."

They headed south, then turned left into an upscale residential neighborhood, and on up into the West Maui Mountains. "So, you think I have ulterior motives?"

"Do you?"

"If I did, wouldn't I be a fool to say so?"

"Maybe we should change the subject," Abby suggested. "Something simple and harmless, like dinner."

And speaking of dinner, she wondered where they were going. The neighborhood was not only strictly residential, but it was beginning to thin out. The farther they drove, the fewer houses they encountered.

"Just where is this restaurant?"

"Don't worry." He whipped the Thunderbird into a tree-lined driveway and braked to a stop in front of a small house. "I'm going to satisfy your curiosity and your hunger at the same time."

"Where? Here?" She eyed the single-story clapboard house, lights glowing from several windows. "Whose place is this?"

She entertained a fleeting hope that they might possibly be joining some friends of his, but the hope was weak at best. In her heart of hearts, she knew the answer even before he spoke.

Houston turned off the engine. "Mine."

"I, uh, thought you said we were eating out in the open?"

He got out of the convertible, walked around to her side and opened the door. "We are." He helped her out. "But first there's that burning question to be answered. Am I, or am I not, a slob?"

"If you say you're not, you're not. I trust you."

"Oh, but Miss Abigail, I don't believe you do."

He took her hand, led her up the front steps, unlocked the door and ushered her inside.

"Wait right here," he instructed, then disappeared. A second later she heard a screen door slam.

The house was immaculate.

And small, but not cramped. She couldn't be certain from where she stood a few feet into the living room, but there were probably only two bedrooms, and one bath. There was a dining nook just off the living room, and if she had to guess, the kitchen was on the other side of the nook. Judging from the size and some of the interior architectural points, she would guess the house had been built in the early fifties. And been very well kept.

Someone—she wondered if it was Houston's handiwork or if he had paid a professional—had gone to great lengths to refurbish the original wood-frame windows and hardwood floors. There was a wide archway with exquisite crown molding leading into the nook, and a similar but smaller one leading into a hallway— presumably toward the bedrooms.

The decor was simple but not plain. And at the risk of sounding clichéd, homey. The walls were painted beige. The trim, including ceiling moldings of the same quality and design as the archways, was painted ivory. A watercolor seascape hung on one wall, and the top of a high narrow table behind the sofa was covered with photographs. The rooms gave the feeling of spaciousness, but at the same time were warm and welcoming.

At the risk of disobeying Houston, Abby walked into the living room and sat down on what appeared to be—judging from the style and fabric—either a sturdy hand-me-down sofa or a great yard-sale find. Either way, it was the central focus of the room, and looked too comfortable to resist.

On first contact, the cushions felt lumpy, but they weren't. Once Abby settled in, the sofa seemed to snuggle up to her body, to get cozy, as if greeting an old friend.

With a deeply satisfied sigh, Abby wiggled her bottom more firmly into the cushion just as Houston walked back into the room.

"Ah, I see you've found my treasure."

"Treasure?"

"You're sitting on it."

"Oh." She smiled, running her fingers lightly over the soft fabric. "It's a great couch."

"Great? It's way past great. I decorated this whole room around it."

Abby glanced around. "I can see that."

"And, I'll have you know, my great-grandmother was sitting on this sofa when my great-grandfather proposed to her."

Well, that answered her question about the sofa's origin. "Now, that is impressive."

"Great-grandmother thought so. She could never bear to part with it, so it resided in my parents' attic for a lot of years. I stumbled over it one day. Literally, I might add. And it just sort of followed me home. So, I kept it."

"Well, I can see why you consider it a treasure."

Houston watched her relaxing, stroking the fabric. Enjoying the comfort he himself had so often enjoyed.

Then a strange thing happened. In his mind's eye he saw
her curled up in a corner of the sofa reading a book,
wearing one of his shirts—and nothing else. He was
sitting at the other end, wearing only jeans. Close
enough to touch her anytime he wanted. Then the picture changed, and he saw her stretched out on the sofa.
Lying there, languid and sleepy-eyed, holding out her
arms to him...

"Houston?"

"What?" he said, a little too loudly.

"For a minute there, you were miles away."

"Not really." He shook off the daydream. "I hope
you brought your appetite with you."

"Now that I see what a whiz you are at housecleaning,
I can't wait to see what's on the menu."

He grabbed her by the hand and tugged her up from
the sofa. "Then follow me."

As he pulled her through the dining nook and the old-
fashioned kitchen, she caught a glimpse of almost-
spotless painted cabinets and countertops. "I thought
you said you were cooking. What did you do with all
the take-out containers, hide them under the sink?"

"You really should learn to be more trusting, Miss
Abigail." He opened the screen door to the backyard.

And she stepped into a fantasy.

The yard was a scaled-down version of a tropical
forest and garden, complete with banyan, date palm,
mango and orchid trees. There were blooming bou-
gainvillea, orange trumpet vines and hibiscus, the flo-
ral emblem of the Hawaiian Islands. To one side was a
fountain and a small pond. Probably recirculating,
Abby decided, but if so, it had been exquisitely created, and appeared completely natural.

And in the center of all this lush beauty was a native
stone patio with a bistro-style wrought-iron table and
two chairs, painted white. The table was set, complete

with a bottle of wine opened to breathe, two candles and a cut-crystal bowl of succulent-looking mixed fruit as a centerpiece.

There was no electric light, only two other sources of illumination. One provided by a heaven full of stars scattered across the black velvet night. The other, candles—dozens of them. Perched on wrought-iron holders stuck into the ground, some were placed around the table, some situated among the greenery and blossoms.

Everywhere Abby looked, above and below, lights twinkled and flickered.

"Whoa," she said, breathlessly. "This is...stunning."

"I was trying to impress you." From a large bush growing beside the back door, he plucked a delicate white hibiscus bloom and tucked it behind her left ear. "How am I doing?"

She looked up at him. "Ex-exceptional. I...I wasn't expecting anything like this."

"Good." He ushered her to the table and seated her. "You ain't seen nothin' yet. Be back in a sec."

As he walked around the corner of the house, out of sight, for the first time Abby realized she heard music. Handel's *Water Music,* if she wasn't mistaken. But where was it coming from? Glancing around, she saw no stereo equipment, no tape player. She decided the speakers must be cleverly hidden somewhere in the foliage.

A second later the most mouthwatering aromas she had ever smelled wafted from the spot where Houston had disappeared. Finally, he reappeared carrying two small napkin-covered baskets, which he set on the table.

He flipped the napkins back to reveal two perfectly roasted Cornish game hens and foil-wrapped ears of corn in one basket, baked potatoes and French bread in the other.

He picked up a slice of the fragrant bread, and passed it beneath her nose. "And that crack about the take-out containers?"

Abby licked her lips, suddenly discovering she was ravenously hungry. "I take it back. In spades."

Houston grinned as he loaded their plates with food. "Now, that's what I like. A lady who knows how to take care of herself. Dig in."

Abby did, and after several minutes of savoring the first few mouthfuls of the delicious food, she dabbed at her chin with a napkin and said, "Practice makes perfect."

"At taking care of yourself?"

"Yes."

"Only child?"

She nodded. "How about you?"

"Two sisters. Both younger."

"I always wanted a big brother."

"Talk to my sisters. They'll convince you fortune smiled on you."

Abby laughed, reaching for the warm bread.

"I like the way you laugh."

"Actually, it's more of a silly giggle."

"Who told you that?"

"My dad."

"At about age five, I'll bet."

"Close."

"Well, lovely Abby, let me assure you . . . Wine?"

"Please."

"Girls giggle. Women laugh. And you," he continued, leaning in close to fill her glass, "have a great laugh."

"Thanks," she murmured. He was so close, and he smelled so good that she had to force her gaze away from his. She concentrated on her meal and small talk.

"I was surprised to see that you live far away from Lahaina."

"Why's that?" The way she tried to keep her distance by changing the subject intrigued him. He was already beginning to learn some of her nuances, and he wanted to learn more.

Abby shrugged. "I suppose I expected you to live in town. Maybe even on the beach since the biggest part of your life has to do with the ocean."

"I used to. But, I decided I liked the peace and quiet up here. And it's a lot cooler."

All of which was true. He didn't tell her that he had considered a beachfront home at one time and was now glad he had decided against it. Because now, he wouldn't have to hear the surf. He wouldn't have to watch the tides coming in. He wouldn't have to remember.

He forked a small chunk of fresh mango, and aimed at her mouth. "Taste this. Came off that tree over there."

"Hmm," she murmured, taking the sweet, pulpy fruit into her mouth. Savoring the exotic taste. "Oh." A drop of juice escaped her lips, and her tongue darted out to capture it.

At the same instant Houston reached a hand to assist.

Her tongue licked his finger.

And both of them jumped as if they had been burned.

"Sorry, I . . ."

"That's . . . all right," Abby whispered, feeling lightheaded. "I just wasn't prepared . . . you know, uh . . ."

"For the mango to be so juicy. Yeah." Lord, but she was something. He couldn't remember ever being turned on this hard or this quick. The feel of her tongue along his finger was like a match rasping against a striker. Only he was the one on fire. "I know."

"It was wonderful. I mean, it tasted great. I can't believe you can just pick fruit from your own trees anytime you want." She was babbling, and she knew it.

"Yeah, it's great. How's your Cornish hen?"

"Delicious. Everything is..." The only word that kept popping into her head was *delicious* because she couldn't stop thinking about the taste of his skin mingled with the juice of the mango. A little salty. A little sweet. And totally, wonderfully delicious. "Everything is really tasty."

"Thanks."

This was dangerous. Far too dangerous. She wasn't supposed to forget she was doing a job, but that was exactly what had happened. She knew better. Lord, did she know better. Yet here she was, gazing across a candlelit table, thinking about how he tasted.

And how she would like to taste him again.

"Can I help with the dishes?"

"Nope." As he rose from the table he deposited the dirty plates and glasses into the now empty baskets. "I'll do these later."

"I really don't mind."

"Absolutely not. More wine?"

"No, thanks." Her head was spinning enough as it was.

"Be right back."

By the time he returned a few minutes later, Abby felt more in control again. "I see you've got a hammock. Is it just for show, or do you use it?"

"Sometimes I sleep out here." He glanced away. "I like looking up at the stars. It's...comforting."

"I've never sat in one."

"You serious?"

"I've seen them in movies and commercials and they look so comfortable, but I've just never had an opportunity."

"Try it out."

"Oh, I wasn't angling to—"

"Go ahead. I'm a firm believer in obtaining the heart's desire whenever possible."

"Well, I wouldn't exactly call it my heart's desire—"

"It's something you've always wanted to do, right?"

"Yes, but—"

"Do it."

Well, Abby admitted to herself, maybe sitting in a hammock under a starry night sky was a secret desire. A tiny one. So, why not?

As with the candleholders and speakers, Houston had gone to some length to hide the metal frame and make the corded bed of the hammock appear to be suspended amid the greenery as if by magic.

He took her hand. "Back up to it, then sit right in the middle. Here." He walked around to the other side and demonstrated.

She followed his instructions, and soon found herself back-to-back with him on the hammock.

"Now, just swing your legs up, and lie back."

She did, and two seconds later was staring up at the stars.

"So, what do you think?" he asked, smiling down at her over his shoulder.

"I love it." She closed her eyes. "One of these is going to the top of my 'must have' list."

Abby was enjoying the experience so much, she wasn't even aware Houston had moved until she felt the other side of the corded bed dip lower. Her eyes popped open.

"What did I tell you?" he said, sliding next to her. "Great, isn't it?"

"Y-yes."

What did she do now? She couldn't very well hop up the minute he joined her. Talk about overreacting. Besides, with her luck, if she tried any quick moves, she would probably wind up dumping both of their butts in the shrubbery.

The trouble was, she wasn't sure she could get up, even if she tried. Because of his weight and size, his side of the hammock was lower. Consequently, her body had followed the law of gravity and rolled smack-dab against his.

They were snuggled up to each other like two proverbial peas in a pod.

Only the big pea had the advantage. He knew how to maneuver on the suspended bed, and he deftly slipped his arm around her, pulling her closer. He nuzzled her earlobe.

"You smell good. What is that?"

"Passion," she said bluntly, wishing she had lied.

He inhaled deeply, exhaled slowly. "I'll say."

With each breath, she watched his chest rise and fall, watched his muscles expand over an already broad chest.

She had admired his body from the beginning, but lying next to him put a whole different perspective on her observation. He was long and lean. Solid.

And warm.

She closed her eyes and savored his warmth. And for a moment, she forgot all about cases and questions. All she thought about was how good it felt to be held in a man's arms again. How much she needed to be held.

But she couldn't afford the luxury of being needy, Abby reluctantly reminded herself. She couldn't afford to forget why she was here in the first place.

But she wanted to. Oh, how she wanted to.

She bit her lip, and told herself to shape up. *Get* up was more appropriate. The longer she let him hold her, the harder it would be to extract herself from this situation. She should just thank him, and ask him to drive her home. That's what she should do.

"Penny?"

"What?"

"For your thoughts."

"I was just thinking that, uh . . . I was thinking that I can see how sleeping out here would be . . . nice."

As confident requests to be driven home went, this one had about as much fizzle as day-old soda pop. "I mean, what could be better than sleeping under the stars?"

Abruptly, there was a subtle change in his body, almost a stiffness. She could feel the vibrations like a discordant note. Vibrations that, despite the fact that he shifted his weight, had more to do with body language than body placement. He was uncomfortable with the subject.

"Do you sleep out here often?"

"A few months back, it was the only place I could sleep."

"When you were renovating? I noticed the windows, molding and floors had been expertly refurbished—"

"I wasn't renovating."

"Oh." She had the feeling he was right on the verge of talking to her, really talking to her. Wanting to point the conversation in the direction of her choosing but knowing it would be a mistake, Abby kept quiet, and hoped Houston would do the rest.

"Abby?"

"Yes."

"You're not planning any more dive trips while you're here, are you?"

What a bizarre question. And a rude one, she thought nastily. "What makes you say that?"

"Are you?" he persisted.

"No," she said, irritated by his strange interrogation.

"Or whale watches?"

Why was he pushing her to admit her fear? It was none of his business and she started to tell him so. Instead, she reminded herself that she couldn't afford to alienate him. But that didn't prevent the edge of anger in her voice.

"No. I'm not planning any more dives, whale watches or snorkel trips. Hell, I may never even go swimming again unless I can see straight to a concrete bottom."

"Because of the shark?"

"Yes," she snapped. Case or no case, he didn't have the right to grill her like this. "I don't want to go back in the water. I . . . I can't. Are you satisfied?" The answer was straight from her heart. Straight out of her fear. "I know you probably think it's irrational."

"Abby—"

"The chances of encountering another shark in my next fifty dives is probably astronomical."

"Abby—"

"I can't explain it. I—"

He turned toward her and cupped her chin in his hand. "You don't have to explain it. I understand."

"How could you—"

"Because," he said on a desperate whisper. "I know exactly what you're feeling. For nine months I've lived with the same fear. And believe me, I would rather have faced your shark than face my own weakness."

He looked deep into her eyes. "I understand, Abby. Because I can't go back into the water any more than you can."

Chapter 7

This was the moment Abby had been waiting for, but she was too stunned to exploit it. She held her breath, knowing he was going to talk about the explosion; knowing he would probably share his feelings. This is what she had come to Maui for, wasn't it?

Then why wasn't she overjoyed?

"There was an accident," he said, as if on cue. "Gil—you met him at the shop—was in Hilo, on the big island. We had been busting our butts to set up a deal with this travel agency on the mainland. Major bucks all the way around. Gil closed the negotiations. I was to sail over and ink the deal, then we were going to celebrate."

He laughed—a humorless, desperate sound. In fact, it raised goose bumps on her skin. "Nobody can paint the town red like Gil." His hand stroked her cheek several times, then he reached to hold her hand. "It would have been a night to remember."

"W-would have been?"

"I never...never made it..." He took a deep breath. "*We* never made it to Hilo."

She waited, knowing he would continue, and strangely enough, wishing he wouldn't. She hadn't expected the raw pain she heard in his voice. She hadn't expected to want to soothe that pain. Would a guilty man be so emotional? Would a guilty man even admit to his fear?

"It was almost sunset," he continued. "The wind had kicked up. Guess it blew us slightly off course. Nothing serious. I think I was correcting, when Shelley..."

At the mention of Shelley's name, his hand held hers more tightly.

"At the last minute Gil's wife, Shelley, decided to come along. She, uh, always went below to make coffee right about sundown. That's where they think she was when..."

He paused for several seconds, then cleared his throat. "There was an explosion. Probably in the galley. A fire. The boat sank. I—I made it to the raft, but Shelley...Shelley didn't. Coast Guard picked me up three days later." He sucked in a breath, and let it out in a slow trickle. "That's all I remember."

His hurry-up-and-get-it-out, bare-bones version of what had happened told Abby more than the reams of reports and depositions she had already read concerning the explosion.

"Except the stars," he said, more to himself than her. "I remember the stars. Every night. Always there."

"Houston?"

"Twinkling. Just twinkling."

"Houston," she said softly. "I'm so sorry. So very sorry."

He hurt. The pain was in his voice, in the tension on his face, even in the desperate way he clung to her hand.

And there was nothing fake or pretend about it. It was all too real. She wanted to put her arms around him and tell him everything would be all right. An absurd notion, given the circumstances, and she knew it.

"They told me I bobbed around in the Pacific for three days with a raging fever. But I don't remember much of that, either."

Abby had read all of the accounts of the explosion, including the reports from the Coast Guard. She had the information in her head. But for the first time it touched her heart. She reached up and stroked his cheek.

She should have been pressing him for details, but all she could think about was how much he must have grieved over the past nine months. She should have felt a certain satisfaction at having finally cracked the door to his emotions. Instead, she empathized.

"Losing someone . . . hurts," she said softly. "When my father died I didn't think the pain would ever go away. And I don't believe it ever completely disappears, but time does take away some of the sting. Some of the tears."

"I hope so. God, I hope so."

"It will. And you have people who care to help you through this. Gil and—"

Abruptly, he swung his feet over the edge of the hammock and sat up, his back to her. "I didn't mean to get into all this," he said into the darkness. "I only wanted you to know that I understood, understand, how you feel."

He was shutting down. Trying to regain control. Coping with the pain the only way he knew how. But the fact that he changed the word *understood* to the present tense, told her he wasn't coping very well.

The only reason Abby recognized the behavior so quickly was because she was intimately acquainted with it herself. Don't share too much of yourself. Don't risk.

"I can see that, and I appreciate it." She reached out to him. "Houston—"

"You're probably curious about the details. It's natural, but . . ."

"But what?"

"I don't remember the details."

"You mean you don't want to think about them. It's understandable, considering all you've been through."

"No, Abby." He twisted his body back around, facing her. "I don't remember. Except for the time leading up to the accident. I remember the sunset and being off course, and then . . ."

The things he remembered most clearly, he would like to forget. God, how he wished he could forget. But how does a man forget he's a coward?

"Most of what I just told you was told to me by the Coast Guard and the insurance investigator. I only remember bits and pieces. The fire. And the stars. But the pieces don't always fit together."

"Traumatic memory loss," Abby whispered. So this was the source of the negative vibes she had picked up from him. This was the something she felt he had been hiding.

"How did you know what it was called?"

She shrugged. "Probably read it somewhere. I don't think this kind of thing is uncommon in situations like yours."

"That's almost exactly what the doctor said that treated me on the Coast Guard cutter."

"I'm sure in time, your complete memory will be restored."

"He said that, too."

"Shall I send you a bill for a second opinion?"

They looked at each other, and both smiled.

"Look." He ran a hand through his hair. "Believe it or not—" he stood, and assisted her exit from the hammock "—this wasn't what I had in mind when I invited you to dinner."

They walked across the yard, and without questioning whether she should be or not, Abby was relieved to move away from the pain she had seen in his eyes.

He opened the back door, and they went inside. "And what did you have in mind?"

"Dinner, and some heavy petting," he answered honestly.

When they reached the living room, she turned and said, "You do that just to throw me off guard, don't you?"

"Do what?"

"Give me such a direct answer."

"Was I supposed to give you an indirect one?"

"You know what I'm talking about."

"If you mean, giving you an honest answer, the answer is no."

Abby frowned. "Now you're trying to confuse me. No, what?"

"No, I don't do it to throw you off. I do it to warn you off." He slid his hand behind her neck, and with very slight pressure, urged her closer. "To protect Little Red from the wolf."

At his touch, her stomach did a couple of cartwheels, disturbing a covey of butterflies. "Do I need to be warned?"

"Oh, yes, Miss Abigail. You most certainly do."

"And . . . and just why do I need to be warned off?"

"That's the way it's always worked in the past. You see—and I'm fully aware that I'm about to sound like a total jerk—being up-front and honest is my technique."

"Technique?"

"Here comes the jerk part. It's been a way for me to keep my past relationships well-defined. And, well, temporary. As long as I was totally honest about what I wanted, the lady couldn't come back later and say—"

"That you whispered sweet promises in her ear. Promises you never intended to keep."

"Exactly. Every woman I've been with knew where she stood. Where we were going."

"And where was that?"

"To have fun, mostly. To bed eventually. But they always knew. I never professed undying love when all I wanted was a good time."

"Well, at least you aren't a cad."

"You missed the most important word in those last couple of sentences."

She tried to hide a smile. "Jerk?"

Houston grinned back, never taking his eyes from hers. His hand cupped her chin. "Past."

Those butterflies in the pit of her stomach were at it again. How was she supposed to respond to him? How did she want to respond to him? Abby tried to derail that particular train of thought, but with little success. Houston was too close, too warm and too…everything.

"You have no reason to believe me, but it's the truth."

"It's not really important whether I believe—"

"Yes, it is."

He could feel her heartbeat beneath his hand, and fought the urge to put his mouth against that soft, pulsing spot. And many, many other places on her body. "It's very important."

Abby knew she shouldn't ask…mustn't ask…. But she asked. "Why?"

"Because I want you."

"That's not exactly news."

"Yeah, but it's how I want you."

"H-how—"

"Hot and fast. Slow and easy. For hours and hours. Days. In the sunlight. Under the stars. And more than I've wanted anyone in a long time."

When her eyes widened, he reminded her, "You asked."

He didn't add that he wanted her sweetness, her smile, her laughter. Everything she had to give. He didn't say those things because, for the present, that admission was almost as unsettling for him to make, as it would be for her to hear.

"You're right. I did need to be warned."

"So, Little Red, now that you know where the Big Bad Wolf lives, do you take your basket of goodies and stay the hell away from Grandma's house?"

"I should." Abby had never spoken truer words. She should—oh, yes—she should get as far away from Houston Sinclair as possible. It was the right thing to do. The sane thing to do. Some part of her brain even told her it was the professional thing to do.

"Don't."

One word. Not a question. Not a command. Not prefaced by the word *please*. Just, "don't."

Slowly, giving her plenty of time to turn away, he leaned closer, dipping his head.

He was going to kiss her unless she stopped him. And she should stop him. Before this got out of hand. All she had to do was tell him to stop. Or even just simply turn her head. There were at least fifty ways to avoid the kiss, and all she needed was one. One simple, little...

Her mouth opened to his, so hungry, so hot.

He took possession of her lips the way he wanted to take possession of her body. Deeply. Completely. Need jumped and sparked inside him like live wires as he feasted on her mouth. He wanted more, needed more.

And he had never felt so alive, so hungry. The hunger gnawed at him, and he pulled her tighter into his embrace, molded her body to his.

Everything in her strained into the kiss, into the heat of it, the power of it. She had never known the kind of searing desire his kiss incited. Her knees were actually trembling. And she wanted more. More, more and more.

Instincts honed by pain demanded she stayed in control. Stayed distant. But need had its own demands. She stopped listening to her instincts. All she heard was her heart as it hammered a primal beat from her body to his.

Her moan of protest when his mouth left hers slid into a sigh as his lips tasted her cheek, her throat. He whispered her name on a ragged sigh right before he nipped at her earlobe.

Her insides felt like liquid fire, her body trembled. She clung to him—his arms for support, his lips for sustenance. At that moment, the center of the universe was their lips, their need.

They were spinning out of control. Both of them seemed to realize it at the same time, and tempered the kiss. Reluctantly.

"Abby." He kissed her temple.

"Don't worry," she said, trying to calm her breathing. "I was warned."

"Only one problem."

"What?"

"Nobody warned me."

"Why?" Her breath came out in a long, shuddering sigh. "I'm harmless."

He laughed. He had to in order to release some of the tension, to rein in his racing libido. "That's got to be the all-time greatest understatement, my lovely—" he kissed her lips, stopping just short of devouring her again "—luscious Abby. At this moment, you're the most dangerous woman on this island." In more ways than one, he thought.

"Dangerous? I've never been called dangerous before. At least not that way."

"Haven't you?" With both hands he caged her face briefly, careful not to dislodge the hibiscus bloom, then slipped them behind her neck, into the mass of curls.

She closed her eyes. "I think I like the idea."

"Do you?" His fingers massaged her scalp.

Her head fell back into his hands in a gesture of surrender that sent desire ripping through his body.

"It's probably every woman's fantasy. To be dangerous, seductive. Maybe not as a steady diet, but at least once. Or once in a while."

"The idea being to keep the males in her life on their toes."

"Something like that, but . . ."

"But what?"

She opened her eyes and looked straight into his. "More to prove to herself that she has what it takes to be dangerous, even if she doesn't use it. Know what I mean?"

"Yeah," he said, only at the moment he couldn't have told her for sure what the question was because his gaze went to her mouth, all soft and waiting to be kissed. He wanted to kiss her again. He wanted to do a lot more than kiss.

Before she had walked into the dive shop, he had considered instant attraction to be synonymous with instant lust. Now he knew different. Not that he wasn't experiencing a healthy dose of lust right now, but Abby was . . . different. Special. And she had been, since the moment he laid eyes on her.

"And—" he sighed "—if I don't take you home right now, you're going to get more than an idea."

"I . . . I think you're right."

He didn't want to, but he took a step back, let her go. "Good thing the top is down. I need all the cool air I can get."

They both got a lot of air as the T-Bird sped down Highway 30, but as for cool . . .

How cool could he be when he couldn't stop thinking about the way her skin tasted, all sweet, and smelling like jasmine? He wanted another taste. More. He wanted to know if the skin on her belly was as soft as that little spot behind her ear. Face it, he thought, she had him tied in knots no sailor ever knew. And some of those knots had nothing to do with sex.

They had to do with the way she had stroked his cheek when she'd told him how sorry she was. They had to do with the gentle way she had tried to console him by sharing about her father.

They had to do with feeling connected to her in a way he had never experienced before.

This was new ground for him. Shaky ground. But at the same time, exciting. Being with Abby had reawakened his adventurer's spirit, almost as if he had been sleepwalking through the past nine months. Now an eagerness flowed through him, as sweet and heady as her perfume.

The air moving over her skin wasn't cool, it was a reminder. A reminder of what was happening to her. Again.

She had removed the hibiscus flower for fear it would blow away as they drove. Now she gazed at it in her hand, wondering how she could have allowed herself to fall into the same trap. Her past experience should have strengthened her emotional protective devices, not weakened them. Every time Houston touched her, she thought less and less about holding on to her objectivity and more and more about holding on to him.

This was insane. She had to pull herself together. Block all these feelings that threatened to swamp her every time she was with him.

"How would you like to take a sight-seeing trip around the island tomorrow? There's some terrific scenery."

"I'd love it." How dangerous can that be, she thought? "I planned on doing a little shopping after breakfast, but I'll certainly be done by ten."

"Let's make it ten-thirty. I'm tied up between nine and ten, and it'll take a few minutes to drive to your place. We can stop for lunch along the road."

"That's fine," Abby said.

If she needed a reality reminder, Houston had just given it to her. Just a little zap to bring her back to her senses, remind her that she was still an investigator, and he was still a suspect.

So, she thought, he would be busy between nine and ten in the morning. The same hour he had been busy this morning when she followed him.

The same hour she would have to follow him again tomorrow.

When he whipped the T-Bird into the parking lot of the condo several minutes later, Abby had regained her composure.

She would play her part but, dammit, she was mad. Foot-stomping mad. At Houston for being so blasted charming that she almost forgot she had a job to do. At herself for forgetting. And madder still at Houston because he had reminded her that she *wanted* to forget. Caught between a rock and a hard place.

Houston helped her out of the car, and walked her to the front door of the condo. "Thanks, Abby," he said when they were standing under the glow of the porch light.

"I think that's my line. Particularly after such a wonderful meal."

"The thanks are for listening."

He sounded so sincere. She didn't want him to sound sincere, grateful or any other damned thing. Being with him was fast becoming an emotional roller-coaster ride. One minute she wanted to cross him off her list of suspects. The next minute she wanted to wring his neck for being a suspect in the first place. And the next minute she was questioning her part in all of this.

Right now, she wanted him to go home and leave her alone.

It cost her, but she had to downplay the intimacy they had shared. "You were just being a good host, trying to make me feel better."

"Abby, I—"

"It was very sweet." She kissed him lightly on the mouth. "Good night, Houston."

"Good night, Miss Abigail."

Glancing at him as she turned to go inside, she pasted on a smile she hoped looked sincere. "Drive carefully."

Once inside, she leaned against the door and sighed. From the instant Houston had mentioned his mysterious disappearing act, she had been antsy to be alone. To be free of the pretending.

She rubbed her forehead where the bud of a headache was threatening to bloom into a real skull pounder, then kicked off her shoes and headed toward the bathroom for some aspirin. On her way, she realized she still held the flower Houston had given her. For a reason she couldn't explain and didn't want to examine too closely, she paused, opened the novel she had been trying to read, placed the bloom inside and closed the book, pressing it between the pages.

When she walked into the kitchen a moment later to get a glass of water, she glanced over at the fax machine.

She had received at least two messages.

From Brax, she wondered? Or maybe responses to the requests for more information. Maybe there was something on one of those sheets that would implicate one of her suspects. Maybe something about Houston?

Clutching two aspirin tablets in the palm of her hand while holding the glass of water with her thumb and index finger, Abby walked over and picked up one of the faxes.

It was a report on Gil Leland's tenure as a San Francisco police officer. She scanned the first two paragraphs and found nothing noteworthy, so she set it aside and picked up the second fax. A very thorough background check on Stuart Baker.

This one was noteworthy. This one had her setting down the glass of water and aspirin. Had her forgetting her headache altogether.

Stuart Baker, aka Stu Barber, Stanley Bell, had a substantial police record.

A criminal record for fraud.

Chapter 8

Holding her third cup of coffee since dawn, Abby stood on the lanai overlooking the tropical garden situated in the center of the condos. She had read the two faxes last night, and again this morning. Part of her was relieved. Part of her was incredibly sad.

She was relieved because, at last, she had information that clearly indicated one of her suspects had the kind of knowledge and experience required to pull off the kind of scam she was investigating. And she was sad because that suspect was Stuart Baker.

The same man who had dealt with her so kindly after her encounter with the tiger shark. The same man who had been so careful not to bruise her dignity or insult her intelligence. How could that man be an arsonist? It didn't make complete sense, yet the information was right there in the fax. Black-and-white, plain English.

"Stuart Baker," using one of his various aliases, had served time in a Florida prison. He and a cohort had been convicted of working a construction scam, bidding on hurricane repair-work that required a hefty down payment. They took the money, and the homeowner never got the work. He and his partner had each served eighteen months of a three-year sentence.

Logically, she reasoned that if he had committed fraud once, he might do it again. And to take logic one step further, what would keep him from deciding it was time to graduate from construction scams to insurance fraud?

So, whether she liked it or not, Stuart Baker had just become her number-one suspect.

A fact that had not gone unnoticed by Brax. At the bottom of Stuart's information was a notation that Brax was requesting a cross-check to see if the Seattle torch and Baker had ever served time in the same jail. Or if they had ever lived in the same city or state. Obviously, Brax's thinking paralleled hers.

Of course, the question of motive still remained. And since Baker didn't stand to gain any of the insurance money, there was only one valid motive that Abby could see.

Revenge.

But what kind? Revenge against Houston or Gil for some wrong they had done? Or possibly one that Baker imagined they had done? She had seen Stuart with Houston and had never noticed any animosity. And from what she could tell, Stuart and Gil were friendly. The guy couldn't be that good an actor.

Since the information on Baker was brand spanking new, Abby tried to rethink the entire scenario. She wanted to approach it in a fresh new way, in light of revenge as a motive. And what she came up with a few minutes later, was a whopper.

Maybe the revenge wasn't directed at the partners at all. Maybe it was directed at Shelley Leland.

What if Baker had fallen in love with the boss's wife? And vice versa. What if she'd had her little fling, then gotten tired of dallying with the hired help and called it quits? And what if Stuart Baker hadn't wanted it to end? Maybe, Abby thought, she was dealing with a classic case of, "If I can't have her, no one can."

Or, what if Baker simply came on to Shelley Leland and she rejected him, then threatened to have him fired?

But none of this jibed with the fact that Abby doubted Baker had the money to pay someone to set the explosives. Of course, if the "someone" was an old cellmate, money wouldn't be an issue. That didn't exclude the time element. How far in advance had Baker, or anyone for that matter, known that Shelley intended to join Houston? Gil was already on Hilo and had been for two days. Just how last-minute was last-minute? Early the same morning of the trip? The night before?

Her questions only seemed to birth more questions. And all the questions brought her back to the details. And details could make or break a case. As unlikely as it might seem at the moment, Abby knew it was possible that once she had the answers, the details would fit together snugly enough to convict.

The first step was to wait and see if Brax found a connection between Baker and the Seattle torch. If they could tie the two together, they would have a solid base on which to proceed.

The only major flaw in Abby's theory was her own perception of Stuart Baker. Try as she might, she just couldn't convince herself that he was capable of murder.

It was her damned instincts again. Were they trustworthy or not? Had she lost her edge, lost her keen sense of being able to read a suspect? The fact that she was asking herself such questions spoke to her still-high level of doubt.

She hated having to analyze herself at every turn, but she couldn't afford to be wrong. There were some very pertinent facts pointing to Stuart Baker's involvement. Weighing those against her recently unreliable instincts, she had to admit that even though he was not her only suspect, he was definitely the hottest.

Then there was the report on Gil Leland.

Abby couldn't put her finger on it, but she had a feeling that there was something missing in all of the information about his career with the San Francisco police. More accurately, something... unsaid. Almost as if the author of the report had deliberately composed it in black-and-white terms. No shadings, no nuances. That fact alone posed questions in Abby's mind.

If her experience had taught her nothing else, it had taught her that human nature plays a role in every investigation. Nothing is ever just black-and-white.

Granted, every police department has policies and procedures, certain formats to deal with the necessary paperwork. And, in all honesty, she couldn't say that the report on Leland contained anything damaging, personally or professionally. There was just something about it that didn't feel right to her.

For one thing, after only a year on the force, he had repeatedly requested, and finally received, a transfer to vice. Shortly after he joined vice, he had gone undercover for over six months. The end result was that he had been one of the key officers in a bust of one of the biggest gambling rings on the West Coast. He had even received a commendation. After that, he had worked vice until he left the department five years later.

By themselves, none of the facts were unusual. But Abby kept remembering Houston's comment the day she first met Gil.

This man will bet on anything.

Was Leland a gambler?

Nothing in any of the background information indicated that he was. If he had been in debt, that fact certainly would have turned up in the original investigation. Besides, if he had needed big bucks to cover gambling IOUs, the size alone would have made the debt extremely difficult to hide. Difficult, but not impossible.

And if Leland had a betting habit, what brand of insanity was it that threw a gambler into close contact with men who were only interested in feeding such a habit? In Abby's experience working with police departments, they were careful to evaluate the men they sent undercover for any areas of weakness—any areas where working undercover could prove to be damaging, and therefore unproductive to the job.

Again, there was nothing in Leland's data that indicated he had any such weakness or propensity. At least, no more so than the average individual. Everybody bought a lotto ticket occasionally, or dropped in to the local bingo parlor.

Abby's stomach growled, reminding her that she needed something more than caffeine. She wasn't done with picking apart the fax on Leland, but it would have to wait until later. At least, she could satisfy herself that something positive had come out of the two faxes.

First, there were only two, not three. And at the bottom of the report on Leland, Brax had written a note: *Sinclair's data unchanged since original investigation. Why waste paper?*

She sighed. Of course, Houston wasn't completely off the hook. There was still his little vanishing act to deal with. And deal with it she must.

Abby wolfed down a quick bowl of cereal, grabbed her purse, and headed off in search of Houston.

This time she parked and waited down the street from the dive shop until he came out, then she followed him.

And was surprised when he pulled into the parking lot of the same recreation center she had noticed the day before. She pulled over across the street and watched.

Houston got out of his car, walked to the back and opened the trunk. He removed several brightly colored plastic rings about the size of a dinner plate, closed and locked the trunk, and went inside the building.

Abby waited a couple of minutes, then got out of her car and walked to the front door. She peered inside the lobby to make sure Houston wasn't where he could see her. Satisfied he was out of sight, she dug into her purse until she found what she was looking for. Then she opened the door and walked up to the woman behind the desk.

"Excuse me." She held up the small notepad. "Mr. Sinclair left this in his car, and I'm pretty sure he'll need it. Can you tell me which room he's in?"

The woman glanced up from her computer printout and looked Abby up and down, then shrugged. "He's where he usually is. In the pool."

"And which way is that?"

"To your right." She returned her attention to the printout. "Around the corner."

"Thanks," Abby said, tucking the now useless notepad back into her purse.

Following the woman's directions, and the splashing noises, Abby arrived at an Olympic-size indoor pool. There were three women sitting and talking at the far end of the pool, but no Houston in sight.

Then she heard a series of childlike squeals mingled with a deep male voice. Off to one side of the large pool was a smaller "baby" pool. Three youngsters, age three or four years, she guessed, were perched on the rim of the pool. A young woman, looking to be in her twenties, with a whistle hanging around her neck, was on the edge beside the kids.

And in the middle stood Houston.

Abby hung back, concealing herself behind a partial wall that shielded the entrance to the rest rooms. She stared, still at a loss as to why Houston was here.

As she watched, he started giving instructions, speaking gently and directly to the children. Then he lifted one of the children, a little boy, onto his tummy in the water, instructing the boy to kick, kick, kick. The child performed the task, and his little friends applauded. Houston set the boy back on the edge of the pool, praising him for a job well-done. Then it was the second child's turn. Then the third. The young woman with the whistle assisted.

Clearly, Houston Sinclair was teaching preschoolers how to swim. But why?

Continuing the instructions, he clasped his hands together, and stretched them out in front of him, demonstrating the ready position to dive. Several times he leaned forward, showing his students how their hands and arms should be when they hit the water.

But Abby noticed that the young woman did all of the underwater demonstrations. Standing in water almost up to his waist, Houston helped the kids with their kicks and strokes. And several times he did demonstrate how to glide.

But without actually putting his head underwater.

And when he finally did, it was to help a scared little boy. Very gently, very patiently, Houston coaxed the child to put his face in the water. They did it together. And both of them came up a little wide-eyed, but proud.

So, that's why he's here, she realized. And why he's kept what he's doing a mystery. He was trying to overcome his fear of the water by teaching these kids how to swim.

Tears blurred her eyes as she watched him with the children. He was trying to take back his life, take back his courage. Working through his own fear by trying to teach kids not to be afraid. Trying—no—doing it, one day at a time.

One tiny stroke, one small kick at a time.

And what better place, or what better support than children? Children—unconditionally accepting, trusting.

The outside world would see nothing strange about his teaching. After all, he was a certified diver. His business centered around water sports and activities. Undoubtedly he was a qualified lifeguard, and trained to teach these wet, wiggling munchkins.

But Abby now knew the real reason.

In that moment, for all intents and purposes, Houston Sinclair ceased to be a suspect in her investigation. The man she was watching humble himself in front of a child could never have committed the kind of violence that had destroyed a boat and taken a woman's life. He didn't have it in him.

Without proof, without anything but her heart as a guide, Abby knew Houston was innocent.

Very quietly and unobtrusively, she left the recreation center and drove back to her condo.

When she opened her front door to Houston forty-five minutes later, she looked at him in a whole new light. He was no longer a suspect. He was just a man. A man she was powerfully attracted to.

"Hi," she said, smiling.

"Ready?"

"For anything."

A half hour later, they were winding their way north on Highway 30, through the mountains, and it was easy to see how Maui had been nicknamed "the valley isle."

Abby soon discovered that Houston's use of the term "terrific scenery" was a gross understatement. The scenery was nothing less than breathtaking.

The road, scarcely more than a trail at some points, took them through peaceful pasturelands, and past lush jungle. It took them through tiny villages tucked quietly away from the mainstream of a busy world. And over passes where a wall of mountain defined one side of the road, and a sheer drop of several hundred yards straight down to a roaring surf defined the other. The word *spectacular* was woefully inadequate to describe the beauty surrounding them.

Deciding that lunch was in order, Houston pulled off the road in what appeared to be an area of thick jungle. No restaurant in sight. Not even a roadside park.

"C'mon," he said, removing a blanket and a picnic basket from the trunk of the T-Bird. "You're going to love this spot. Gotta do some climbing, but it's worth it. This place has got everything. A great breeze, and a view to die for."

She eyed the narrow path he indicated, almost overgrown with vegetation. "You're sure?"

"Trust me."

The sixty-four-thousand-dollar question, Abby thought, as she followed him. Now that she was almost certain that Houston was innocent of any wrongdoing...

Almost?

Call it an old habit, credit it to years of training and experience, but she couldn't completely dismiss the possibility—although she wanted to—that even though Houston didn't commit the crime, he might have known about it.

But something inside Abby rejected even that much incrimination. She couldn't get the image out of her mind of Houston coaxing the frightened boy, and him-

self, to face their fear. While her experience had taught
her to never dismiss a suspect without positive proof, it
had also taught her to be a good judge of character.
Plus, he seemed so much more relaxed since he had told
her about not being able to go back in the water. Undoubtedly, her vibes about him hiding something had
been right. The something was his fear.

Maybe her feelings were clouding her judgment, but
she honestly didn't think so.

After a rigorous ten-minute climb, Abby received a
bit of reassurance that Houston was as good as his
word. But once again, he was guilty of understatement.

The "spot" was a plateau, lush green and dotted with
blooming trees, fitted into the side of the mountain. A
delicious breeze stirred the trees, and behind them a
high narrow waterfall cascaded into a small pool.

"It looks like a picture postcard," Abby said when
she got her first glimpse of the beautiful serene glade.

"If it isn't on one, it should be."

"How in the world did you find it?"

"Purely by accident." He took her hand and started
leading her across a line of rocks that formed a step-
ping-stone path across the pool. "And I'm not the least
bit ashamed to say that I've kept it all to myself."

"You mean you don't bring all your dates up here?"

"You're the first."

Abby stopped, almost losing her balance. "Seriously?" she asked, teetering atop a huge rock.

"Seriously."

Still holding her hand, Houston tugged gently. "I'm
starving. How about you?"

Only for the way he was looking at her, Abby
thought. Only for the way she felt when she was with
him, which was wonderful.

When they made it to the other side of the pool, he spread the blanket in the shade of a kukui tree, and opened the picnic basket. It was loaded with fresh fruit, French bread, cold baked herbed chicken and a thermos; plus paper plates, plastic utensils and napkins. Everything the well-dressed picnic required.

While they ate, Houston pointed out and named several varieties of birds and foliage. The glade was so calm and lovely, it reminded her of his little piece of paradise at his home.

Abby licked the last traces of the tasty meal from her fingers. "You modeled the landscaping in your backyard after this place, didn't you."

"Bright girl," he replied, then stretched out on the blanket, his hands behind his head, eyes closed. "I could drift off so easily right now."

"A full stomach has that effect." She polished off the last few grapes.

"That, and very little sleep."

"Did you have a bad night?"

"I've had worse."

She put the untouched food back into the hamper. "What's the matter? Too many lumps in your pillow?"

"It wasn't the pillow. It was you."

She halted in the middle of brushing bread crumbs off the blanket. "Me?"

"Yeah, you. That is to say, thinking about you. Wanting you."

"You're doing it again."

He opened one eye. "Doing what?"

"That direct thing. Are you still trying to warn me off?"

Houston sat up, took her by the shoulders and kissed her full on the mouth. His tongue did wild, wicked things that set her mind spinning and her heart racing.

The kiss was powerful, possessive, making erotic promises she longed for him to keep.

"Does that feel like a warning?" he asked, when they came up for air a moment later.

Abby's breath came out as a ragged sigh. "Only if you're warning me to expect more of the same."

Grinning, he lay back and closed his eyes again. "See how that direct thing works."

Oh, she saw how it worked, all right. It worked to his advantage because it kept her off guard. Because it made her think about what it would be like to have more of those kisses, more of him. God, but he was charming, she thought, stretching out beside him.

"So, how long do we have in this idyllic little spot?" she asked.

"How does the rest of the year sound? Maybe even the decade."

"You mean you took the whole day off?"

"It's cool. Gil is handling today's whale watch, along with Lonnie. And as for the store, Stuart has everything under control."

Stuart.

Abby's spirit nosedived. She didn't want to think about Stuart Baker. Not here in this exquisite setting. She didn't want to ruin an otherwise stunning day with thoughts of him behind bars. Which was most certainly where he would end up if he was responsible for blowing up the *Two of a Kind*. But most of all she didn't want such thoughts to intrude on her time with Houston.

The admission was shocking, and extremely revealing at the same time.

Since the moment she had begun to think of Houston as innocent, her feelings for him had changed. Or rather, intensified. She knew it. She even had an inkling of what lay in store when—not if, but when—the attraction took its natural course.

She just didn't know what she was going to do about it.

"You're mighty quiet."

Abby opened her eyes to find him propped on one elbow, gazing down at her. "Restful."

"Hmm."

"I thought you were zonked out."

He shook his head. "Thinking."

"About what?"

"About the fact that you and I have shared two meals, several toe-curling kisses, and even..." His voice softened when he added, "an intimate, soul-to-soul moment or two. But other than the fact that you live in L.A., I don't know anything about you."

"There's not much to know," she answered, hating the fact that she was undoubtedly about to dump another lie on him.

Idly, Houston played with a strand of her hair. "What do you do for a living?"

"I work for a fact-finding agency," she stated the half-truth.

"You mean like research?"

"Something like that."

"What kind of research?"

"Statistics, mostly. It's not very exciting." At least not anymore, she thought. At the moment, she wished that she could honestly tell him she worked as a receptionist at her dentist's office. "Not nearly as exciting as living a short distance from places like this."

"It has its moments." He smiled. "Like now."

"Far cry from Texas, huh?"

Mentally she was dancing as fast as she could to move the conversation away from her career. Hopefully, away from her, personally, altogether. But he wasn't cooperating.

"Yep. So, you got family in L.A.?"

"Just my mom."

"No siblings?"

"'Fraid not. You said you had sisters, right?"

"Right. C.C.—excuse me, Cecile—the oldest, is divorced, and teaching at Harvard." He mimicked a Boston accent. "Janine still lives in Houston, married to a stockbroker, and raising a passel of kids."

"That sounds nice," she said, wondering how different her life might have been if she'd had more family.

"As the youngest, and the only boy, I didn't think so when I was growing up. But they're great ladies. Good-looking, funny. And smart."

"You're proud of them."

"Yeah, I am."

"And they're probably just as proud of their baby brother."

Houston almost winced, remembering the way his parents and sisters had flown in to be with him while he was hospitalized. He couldn't bear the thought of them knowing about his cowardice.

He frowned, and several seconds ticked by before he answered. "I'm not so sure about that."

"Why? You have a very successful business. And I know that kind of success doesn't just happen. It takes plenty of hard work."

"Lately, I haven't felt as if I've been pulling my fair share of the load. But I'm trying to change that."

"And you will," she assured him. What she really wanted to tell him was that she knew how hard he was trying. She wanted to tell him how proud she was, how wonderful he was for facing his fear—something she couldn't do. She couldn't even entertain the idea of another dive anytime soon. Maybe never.

"You've got more courage than I do."

Houston knew she meant it as a compliment, but the word "courage" made his insides twist into a knot. He sat up.

"You know, I promised you a tour of the island, and we're not getting very far sitting here."

His abrupt change of subject surprised her. "Can it get any better than this?"

"Sure. There are some killer falls not far from here, and a stretch of coast where the surf breaks within a few yards of the road. Spectacular." He stood, and offered her a hand up.

"All right." He pulled her to her feet.

Negative vibes, similar to the ones she had gotten before, were zinging through her. Similar to the ones that had told her he was trying to hide something. But she knew about his hydrophobia. What else could he have to hide?

She studied him as he gathered up the blanket and picnic supplies. Unless she was reading more into the situation than existed, Houston was tense. Not the tight-muscle variety, but that underlying kind of tension that comes from a nagging worry. It was there around his eyes, his mouth.

One thing was certain: it hadn't been there when he kissed her; it hadn't been there when they talked about her. It had only appeared after he became the focus of the conversation.

After a few minutes of pondering as she followed him back to the car, Abby gave up trying to figure it out and concentrated on keeping up with his long strides. Another curiosity. He seemed to be in a hurry to leave, whereas only a short time ago, he'd been willing to spend—did he say, decades?—in the little hideaway glade.

They resumed their trip, and to her surprise, Houston's tension faded. In no time, he was his charming self again. But she noticed that he kept the conversation light, concentrating on the scenery.

Because they had gotten such a late start, Abby had to be satisfied with only a tour of the northwest end of Maui. They drove through Honokohau Bay, Waihee, on to Kahului where the main airport was located, then took Highway 380 back across the north-central part of the island to connect with Highway 30.

"I had planned on taking you to dinner tonight," Houston said as they headed back toward Lahaina. "But I forgot about the game."

"Game?"

"Yeah. A bunch of guys get together occasionally for a few hands of poker."

"Sounds so...masculine," she teased.

"Anyway, I forgot that the game is tonight."

Was it really? she wondered. Or was the game a handy excuse for him to gain some distance. "That's all right."

"How about breakfast?"

"Love to."

So much for that theory. Maybe this poker party was on the up and up. As much as a basically illegal game can be on the up and up.

"So, I don't suppose you guys play for matchsticks, huh?"

"Bite your tongue, woman. You can't say real men and matchsticks in the same sentence."

"Oh, is that how it is?"

"Yeah, you know. Male bonding."

"I've heard of the phenomenon."

An idea popped into Abby's mind, and she realized the opportunity was too good to let it pass. Stuart Baker might be her number-one suspect, but she wasn't ready to completely dismiss Gil Leland. And of course, there was always the possibility that Baker and Leland were working together.

"Is this a regular game?"

"Sort of. It's a floating game, but the same people don't show up every week. Mostly guys that work at the harbor. A couple of them are tour operators. The rest are just guys we hang around with. We're not talking Las Vegas, here. Strictly small change. I doubt there's ever a bet made over ten dollars."

"Do you play often?"

"Not really, but Gil gets a kick out it. Every once in a while he drags me along with him."

"That's right. You told me that he'd bet on anything."

"Let's just say it's a good thing gambling's not legal in Hawaii."

"That bad?"

"Well, to be perfectly honest, sometimes he has a problem with gambling. He has to watch himself or he won't know when to quit."

Her earlier idea had now taken on a life of its own, conjuring up questions, suppositions, despite the fact that in the back of her mind Abby knew she could be way off base on this. Illegal poker games were as common as stray cats. Just because Gil Leland frequented one, and had a tendency not to know when to stop, didn't mean that he had an addiction. If—and she had to admit it was a big if—he was addicted, that didn't mean he was so far in debt that he would be desperate to get out. Desperate enough to take drastic measures to resolve the problem.

But it was possible, even plausible. The more she thought about it, the more the idea took root. She felt a desperate need to fit the pieces of the puzzle together; a drive to pursue Gil as a strong suspect.

When Houston dropped her off at her condo, he gave her a lingering goodbye kiss, and promised to call later. Truthfully, Abby wasn't totally disappointed. She had some thinking to do.

Chapter 9

Try as she might, Abby couldn't shake the notion that Gil Leland's days as a cop working vice, and his penchant for gambling were not only connected, but pointed to a motive. Her theory, such as it was, centered on the assumption that if the sum owed was large enough, it was motive enough.

As hunches went, it was flimsy. She had no proof, and she wasn't sure she could get any. But the more she thought about it, applying her offbeat brand of logic, the more it made sense. To her, at least.

Beginning with the assumption that Leland's yen for cards or dice was strong enough to leave heavy-duty IOUs with someone. But who?

Rob Gunderson was no slouch. He would have sniffed out any sizable debt during the original investigation. Logic dictated that if the debt had existed at that point without Gunderson's knowledge, it was incredibly well hidden.

Who could hide that kind of debt? And why?

At this point, logic posed another question. If Leland had a tall stack of IOUs floating around out there somewhere, where did he get the money to hire a torch?

Of course, the torch could have done the job with a down payment and a promise of more when the insurance company paid off.

And how much money could he lose in a local poker game, anyway? What had Houston called it? "Strictly small change." That certainly didn't sound like the kind of amounts someone killed for. But stranger things had happened.

Once again, Abby reminded herself that when it came to money, people were rarely predictable. And if the amount was large enough, they were prone to do things totally out of character and diametrically opposed to their nature.

But that was the trouble with her theory regarding Gil. She didn't see how losing, even losing consistently at a small-change poker game, could have gotten him far enough in debt to make him desperate. Theoretically it was possible, she supposed, but even theoretical supposition brought you back to the same place. Any debt of that magnitude would have turned up originally.

No, in order for her theory to work, Leland would have to have suffered massive losses. Big bucks. And if Gil had an addiction, he probably didn't limit himself to a friendly poker game once a week.

Pacing the small living room of the condo, Abby ran her hand through her hair. Okay, so there were a few holes, but her theory would hold together eventually. It had to.

She had to find the answers to all the questions stomping around in her head. She had to pull all the facts together into some semblance of order. Abby thought about going over the file again. She had never been completely free of the feeling that she had missed something; that the key to solving the puzzle, answering all the questions, was somewhere in the file. It was there. She just kept missing it.

Yes, she'd go over the file with a fine-tooth comb again. And again if she had to.

It didn't matter if she had to go over the damn file fifty times. She *had* to tie up all the loose ends in this case so she could prove . . . prove . . .

Suddenly she stopped pacing. Just exactly what was she trying to prove?

Abby stood very still, listening to the sound of her own heart as it beat an accelerated rhythm. She was wound up like an eight-day clock. What the hell was wrong with her?

In the last twenty-four hours she had gone from listing Stuart Baker as her number-one suspect, to now going after Gil Leland. And even though she knew her suspicions weren't without validity, none were strong enough to produce this . . . this drive to establish one of them as the arsonist.

Looking back, she realized there was a frantic quality to her reasoning where these two men were concerned. Almost a desperation to nail one of them. Close the case. A hell-bent, burning need to prove one of them was guilty.

And in doing so, prove Houston innocent.

Abby took a deep breath and let it out slowly. Then she opened the sliding-glass door to the lanai and stepped out into the sultry night. Leaning against the railing that overlooked the garden and courtyard, she stared out toward the sea. Even from here, she could hear the surf pounding against the beach.

"What am I doing?" she asked the night. "Am I crazy?" Her only response was the silent twinkling of the stars.

Crazy or not, it was clear to her now that her almost-frenzied scramble to settle this case was not to prove guilt, but to exonerate Houston. To prove that he could never have committed such a violent crime. And all because something inside her insisted he was gentle, kind, and basically honest. Because he had courage and integrity. Because...

Because she cared about him.

"Oh, no," she whispered, her hands suddenly flying to her mouth as if to prevent any other such revelations from escaping her lips.

She cared about Houston.

It was as simple as that. And as complicated.

Talk about understatements. "Complicated" didn't even begin to cover it. How could this have happened, she asked herself? How could she have allowed her feelings for Houston to influence her job? After all the promises she had made to herself.

Ask a stupid question, Abby thought. It happened because she couldn't maintain a decent defense against all that charm. It happened because she got suckered in, just like she had with Riley.

No. No, that wasn't completely true. Houston wasn't Riley. He wasn't anything like Riley.

Abby sighed. If there was any comfort to be had, it was in the fact that at least her feelings were out in the open. Here she was, facing the one thing she had dreaded from the very beginning, the one thing she had worked so hard to prevent happening, and she was still standing. Evidently, she hadn't learned her lesson. The question now was, what did she do about it?

"Nothing," she insisted. The stars didn't argue.

There was nothing she could do. Not without jeopardizing the case. And she couldn't do that. She couldn't turn her back on the trust Brax had placed in her. But neither could she turn her back on Houston.

For the present, the only hope she had was not to act on her feelings for him. She had to keep a clear head, and keep her distance.

But how did she accomplish that feat when she wanted to be with him? Wanted him to touch her, hold her.

The phone rang, and she hurried to answer it. "Hello."

"I didn't wake you, did I?" Houston asked.

"No." Great. All she had to do was hear his voice, and her heart started to beat faster.

"I was afraid you might have gone to bed early or something."

"No, I, uh... I was trying to finish a novel I brought with me." Weak, Abby thought, but better than telling him she had just been hanging around, thinking of him.

"Good one?"

"I suppose," she said, racking her brain for what she could remember of the plot. "One of those, uh, stories where the heroine saw a murder, and now she's in danger, and the hero sort of gets trapped into saving her."

"They don't like each other very much, but they can't keep their hands off each other. One of those?"

"Yeah." Was it her imagination, or had his voice dropped, softened?

"Sexy, huh?"

"Depends on your definition of 'sexy,' I suppose."

" Remind me to give you my definition sometime. Soon."

"Did, uh... Was there some reason you called, other than checking out my reading material?"

"Breakfast. What time shall I pick you up?"

Here was her opportunity to put some distance between them. All she had to do was turn him down. Politely but firmly. "I, uh, I've been thinking. You know, maybe I'm taking up too much of your time. You've got a business to run, and—"

"Abby."

"I just don't want to monopolize all of your time—"

"Abby?"

"Yes."

"Do you want to have breakfast with me?"

There was a long pause until she finally admitted, "Yes." Some opportunist she was. One direct question, and she folded like a cheap card table.

"Then, what time?"

"Oh. Well, whatever time is convenient for you. I mean, I don't know your schedule, so—"

"I'm an early riser."

"Me, too."

"I like to hit the shower by seven, and get on with the day."

"Seven," she murmured, visualizing water streaming down his naked body, slick and warm. Over those wonderfully broad shoulders, down over his tight, shapely butt.

"How about eight? That okay with you?"

"S-sure. Fine. Eight is fine."

"And maybe we can take in Whaler's Village afterward."

"Sounds good."

"Well . . . guess I'd better let you get back to your book."

"Thanks. S-see you in the morning."

"Sweet dreams, Miss Abigail."

Abby stared at the phone for moments after he hung up.

"Coward," she said, finally. "You had your opportunity, and you blew it."

Tomorrow she would have to make a concerted effort to keep things cool between them. She could do it. All she had to do was remember what was at stake, here. What she stood to lose if they got . . . involved.

Define "involved," she thought. As in enjoying his kisses? As in thinking about him constantly? As in wondering what kind of lover he would be? That kind of "involved"?

If she was honest with herself, Abby had to admit that she was well past the involvement stage. The best she could hope for was containment of the situation. She just needed to remember that tomorrow, when Houston was being his usual charming self.

She walked over to the table she had been using as a desk. The file lay open, with her handwritten notes and show-and-tell list beside it. One thing that couldn't wait until tomorrow was sending a fax regarding Leland. Brax was probably going to think she had lost her mind, but she knew he would do his best to get the data she needed as quickly as possible.

And she needed to know if Gil Leland had any outstanding gambling debts anywhere.

Abby was up long before seven, dressed and waiting. Nervously waiting. This is insane, she told herself, but that didn't prevent her from checking her makeup at least three times, and fussing with her hair unnecessarily. It didn't prevent her from agonizing over what to wear, finally settling on a soft cotton sundress with thin straps that crossed at the back—after changing no less than twice. By the time Houston knocked on the door, her stomach was tied in knots. She was not the cool, collected person she had planned to be.

"You look great," he said when she opened the door.

She wanted to tell him the same thing, but just said, "Thanks."

Actually, he looked better than great dressed in khaki walking shorts, a white safari shirt and sandals. Actually, he was so handsome, she felt a little weak in the knees just looking at him.

"Ready?" He held out his hand and she took it.

"As I'll ever be."

They ate breakfast at a small restaurant not far from the condo, then headed for Whaler's Village.

"Since the real deal is not an option," Houston said as they went inside the museum, "I thought you might enjoy seeing the same kind of stuff the tourists see on a whale watch. They've got a great video in here about the humpbacks, including their songs."

"Do they really sing?"

"Like a bird." She cut him a disbelieving glance. "Well, maybe like a bird with a very deep voice."

"Cute."

"Early sailors used to hear it through the hulls of their boats. Lone Star uses hydrophones on all our cruises so the tourists can hear it for themselves. And we run slide presentations in the evenings at several of the resorts." He pointed her toward a small viewing theater. "Did you know only the male sings?"

"Oh, boy, the macho thing really runs the gamut, doesn't it."

"Give me a break. He sings when he's courting his lady whale."

"Seriously?"

"Seriously," he insisted.

She wasn't certain, but a few seconds later she could have sworn she heard him half whispering, half singing the first few bars of "Some Enchanted Evening."

They easily found good seats in the sparsely-filled theater.

"Did you bring the popcorn?" he asked, as soon as they settled in their seats.

"No. And be quiet." Lights dimmed, and the music came up. "The film is about to start."

"How can you expect me to watch a flick without popcorn? Isn't there some kind of law about that?"

Abby put her finger to her lips. "Shh."

"Do that again."

"What?"

"That shushing thing."

Before she thought, Abby pursed her lips and raised her index finger.

But Houston interceded. And what a way to intercede. He captured her finger and kissed her. There, in front of at least a dozen museum visitors, he just kissed her.

"I've been wanting to do that ever since I picked you up."

"And you needed an excuse?"

He grinned. "No, an opportunity. That restaurant was way too public to suit me."

"Oh, and this is what you call 'private'?"

"No," he said, his voice husky. "I just couldn't wait any longer."

As a narrator began to tell the viewers about the beauty and grace of humpback whales, Abby scarcely heard over the drumming of her wildly beating heart.

The man was point-blank honest, and dangerously charming. And she was in big trouble.

She tried to focus on the narration, but just about the time she thought she had it under control, Houston put his arm around her shoulder. Her breath hitched, and she swallowed hard. That was when she realized he wasn't watching the screen, he was watching her.

"You're not paying attention," she whispered.

"I know this stuff by heart."

Of course, he knew the information by heart. It was his job to know. "We don't have to stay."

"That's okay." His hand moved to caress the back of her neck. "I'm enjoying myself."

"Y-you're sure?"

He leaned close and whispered in her ear, "Positive."

Abby was positively a nervous wreck by the time the film was over, and she couldn't have recapped anything the narrator said, if her life depended on it. The only thing she knew for sure was that Houston had touched, stroked and caressed her neck and shoulders thoughout the entire film.

And she had loved every heart-pounding, nerve-racking, delicious second.

"I wish you could see one of these things in the water," Houston said as they stood gazing at a bronze replica of a mother humpback and her calf located in another wing of the museum.

"Maybe I will. Someday."

"For the last two hundred years they've been coming to the warm waters of Hawaii to breed, and give birth. They're magnificent in the open sea."

"Have you ever swum with whales?"

"Once. And I can tell you it was as much a spiritual experience as it was physical. Like nothing I've experienced before or since. But I didn't do it here. You can't. In 1988 they passed a series of laws that restrict any activity near the whales."

"But that's good."

"Yeah. The North Pacific herd of humpbacks has dwindled from fifteen thousand to about two thousand. Fortunately, conservation is popular at the moment, and the situation is looking better."

It was obvious to her that his interest and concern went deeper than simply how it affected his business. He had a genuine appreciation for the ocean and its creatures, all its mystery and splendor.

They moved on to see the nineteenth-century scrimshaw exhibit, and whaling artifacts offered on the third level of the museum. Also, miniature replicas of whaling vessels. Abby stopped briefly in one of the many shops in the village to buy some postcards and a small gift for her mom. Houston left her to her browsing and was gone for about fifteen minutes before returning. Other than that brief time, he never left her side. And through it all, he either held her hand or kept his arm around her shoulder. Once, he even brought her hand to his lips and kissed it.

She wasn't accustomed to such intimacy, but it was comforting in a way she couldn't explain. It shouldn't be, she warned herself. Where was her backbone? Where was all the containment she was supposed to be maintaining? All she knew for certain was that by the time they finished with Whaler's Village, she was returning his little touches with her own. And it felt good, so good.

"I'm starved," he announced. "How does pizza grab you?"

"With or without anchovies?"

He wrinkled his nose. "Without."

"It definitely grabs me."

"Great. Let's get take-out, and go back to your condo."

The request was so unexpected, Abby almost balked. Quickly, she took mental inventory of her living room. No notes scattered about. No files on the table. The only question mark in her mind was how was she going to be able to turn off her fax machine without Houston knowing. "Sounds terrific," she said at last, knowing there was no graceful way to refuse.

They ordered, and picked up a giant pizza, discovering he liked green olives, and she liked black. They both nixed the onions.

When they stepped inside her condo, the first thing they noticed was the strains of lovely Hawaiian music coming from somewhere outside her lanai.

"Uh, why don't you get us a couple of soft drinks from the refrigerator, and I'll clear off the table," she said.

While he headed to the kitchen, she set the box of pizza on the table, then picked up the arrangement of fresh flowers sitting in the center and moved it to the combination credenza and entertainment center on the wall across from the sofa. Quickly, she yanked open the door of the credenza's left-hand cabinet and flipped the Off switch on the fax machine, which she'd stored there with her paperwork, out of sight.

Then she walked to the sliding-glass door, opened it, and stepped outside. "Oh, look. They're giving hula lessons in the courtyard."

Houston set the two soft drinks on the table beside the box of pizza, and came to stand behind her. "Hmm." He slipped his arms around her, leaned in close, and kissed her temple. "You smell like sunshine and sea air."

"She's incredibly beautiful," Abby said of the teacher.

"Hmm. I don't recognize her, but she's good. Excellent, in fact."

Abby looked at the beautiful Polynesian instructress, her supple body moving gracefully to the music, her fluid hand motions telling a story. The woman was exotic, alluring. The kind of woman Houston, or any man for that matter, would undoubtedly find attractive. She wondered how many women he had known, loved.

"Do you know a lot of the native... teachers?"

His chin almost resting on the top of her head, Houston smiled. "Jealous?"

"Of course not. I—"

"Yeah, I know a few hula teachers, a couple of singers, some flight attendants, a secretary or two."

"Are you acquainted with every beautiful woman on this island?"

"However many I know, or have known, the number increased by one a few days ago. A very special one," he said, a second before his lips claimed hers.

She turned completely in his arms, wanting his kiss, needing it. In fact, she realized she had been wanting exactly this very thing all morning.

She shouldn't be wanting it, enjoying it. Wanting more. Oh, but she did.

"Come inside," he whispered against her mouth, and she followed him without protest.

The instant the door closed behind them, he curled his fingers into her hair to drag her mouth back to his.

"The pizza will get cold," she said between kisses.

"Let it."

He made a sound deep in his throat as he used his lips to rub hers apart. His tongue went searching inside her mouth, marauding. Abby moaned, pressing herself to him, glorying in the kiss.

Houston's arms slid around her waist, pulling her even tighter against him, conforming her body to his. One hand slipped down to cup her fanny.

Somewhere in the still-rational recesses of her mind Abby knew she was supposed to be keeping her cool, her distance. She was supposed to be remembering that involvement with a suspect brought disastrous results. But at the moment, she couldn't think of anything more disastrous than not having his kiss, not having his arms around her. Not having him.

"Abby, Abby." He tore his mouth from hers, pressing it against her neck. With both hands in her hair, he pulled her head back, and stared into her face. "You're driving me crazy, you know that?"

"I think I do." Only because he was doing the same to her. Only because if this was insanity, they could lock her up and throw away the key.

"You're always in my thoughts. My dreams."

"Am I?"

"Yeah. I woke last night in a cold sweat from wanting you."

He kissed her again, thoroughly, taking what he wanted and giving more than she ever expected. His tongue stroked her mouth in a purely sexual rhythm. And when his mouth did leave hers, it was to plant tiny kisses on her neck and shoulders, dislodging one of the straps holding up the bodice of the sundress.

"Your skin is incredible. So soft."

Abby sighed, tunneling a hand through his hair when he kissed the swell of her breasts. She didn't think anything could feel as good as his lips on her skin. She didn't want it to stop, didn't want—

The ringing of the phone shattered the quiet intimacy. Reluctantly, they broke apart.

"Sure you want to answer that?" He nibbled at the tender spot behind her ear.

"It could be important."

"So is this."

There were only two people who knew she was here. Brax and her mother. "It could be my mom," Abby said, still breathless. There was a possibility her mother would be on the other end of the line, but in the back of her mind, she doubted it.

"Then I guess you'd better take it."

"Guess so." She slipped out of his embrace.

"Hello," she said a second later.

"Well, finally," Brax said. "I've been trying to reach you for the last half hour—"

"Hi, Mom. Sorry, I missed your call. I've been out all morning."

"You're not alone."

"Right, uh-huh." She smiled at Houston, hating the fact that she had to play out this charade. "I wouldn't want to miss a thing. Yes. It's everything you ever read about and more."

"One of the charm boys?" Brax surmised.

"Absolutely."

"Call me back when he leaves."

"Sure, Mom. I'll give you a call with the flight number. Love you, too. Bye." She looked at Houston apologetically and shrugged. "Just checking up on her baby girl."

Houston came over to her, took her hand and lifted it to his lips for a tender kiss. "Her baby girl is in good hands."

"Yeah, well. You know how mothers are." She glanced away, feeling awkward.

"Relax." He slipped an index finger under the fallen strap and eased it back onto her shoulder. "She can't see through the telephone."

Abby grinned, and jumped at the easy out he had unknowingly offered. "Guess we're all still kids when we deal with parents. All those old rules just pop right to the surface again. Like it's up to you to make sure guys respect you. You know," she said, linking her hands together in an almost-childlike way. "Stuff like that."

Houston leaned over and kissed her cheek in a very tender, gentlemanly fashion. "Yeah. Stuff like that."

"We, uh, never did get to the pizza."

"I'm not really hungry anymore." Not for food, anyway, he thought, gazing at her mouth. But he didn't intend to press the issue after seeing how skittish she was after the phone call.

"There's a microwave in the kitchen. I guess we could, uh— "

"Heat it up?"

"If. . . if that's what you really want."

"What I want," he said, stroking her cheek with the back of his hand, "is to make love to you. . . ."

Abby held her breath.

"When it's right. Right place. Right time. I won't lie and tell you it wouldn't have happened today, but for that call."

"I'm—"

He touched a finger to her mouth. "You wanted it as much as I did."

Abby licked her lips. "Yes."

He placed his thumb beneath her chin to tilt it up. "We're going to be good. You know that, don't you?"

"Yes." She knew they would be better than good.

"The anticipation only makes it sweeter." He kissed her quickly, then walked to the door. "Will you go to dinner with me tonight?"

"Yes."

"Pick you up at eight?"

"Yes."

He blew her a kiss, and left.

Abby stared at the closed door for a long time, wanting to call him back. Wanting to call back the moment, his kiss, everything. Everything she'd had before the phone call.

Brax's call. Abby sighed.

She went to the cabinet in the credenza and flipped the On switch to the fax machine. Then she picked up the phone and dialed the office number.

Brax answered immediately. "Hall, here."

"Sorry about that, but I couldn't talk."

"I got your drift. How come I couldn't reach you by fax?"

"I turned the machine off. My guest might have thought it a bit odd for someone on vacation to bring their fax machine with them."

"Oh, yeah. Smart girl."

"Thanks."

After a pause he said, "Aren't you going to ask what was in the message you didn't receive?"

"Sure. What was it?"

"Nothing...now," he said, clearly put off.

"What do you mean?"

"Well, Leland did owe some sizable dollars to some people in Las Vegas. We're talking major bucks, here."

"Did?"

"Yeah. He paid up. Same goes for a bookie in Lahaina and one in Hilo. Looks like we struck out."

"Great. Any idea where he got that kind of money?"

"Nope. Not so far, but we'll keep checking. How you doing on your end?"

"So-so."

"You know, Miss Abigail, we may have come to a dead end on this one. It's possible."

"I don't think so. I've still got the feeling that we—that everybody—has overlooked something."

"Maybe you're right. But we're running out of time. We can't stay on this forever, if we don't come up with something substantial."

"I know."

"Well, guess you can hang in there for a while longer. Let me know what's happening."

"I will."

"And don't turn off that damn machine again," he ordered.

"I won't," she assured him and hung up.

Brax was right, Abby thought. She was running out of time.

In more ways than one.

Chapter 10

She thought about canceling the date several times throughout the day. She thought about it, but she couldn't bring herself to do it. She couldn't because, truthfully, she didn't want to. Truthfully, she wanted to be with Houston.

She'd done some stupid, careless things in her life, and this ranked right up there with the worst of them. For all her determination not to allow herself to become emotionally dependent on Houston, she had done precisely that.

The problem was, now she wouldn't have it any other way. Now, she knew the truth. She was in love with him.

When it had happened, she wasn't sure, but there was no doubt about it. She loved him.

And he was right. They would be good together. They would be great, if only...

"If only he forgives you for being a liar," Abby said out loud.

Just a minor difficulty. All she had to do was tell him the truth.

Oh, yes. The truth. That she had come to Maui to investigate him. That she had lied from the start. But not to worry. She didn't think he was guilty. In fact, she was willing to stake her professional reputation on his innocence. Oh, and by the way, she thought his partner was guilty as sin. That he had probably paid someone to blow up the boat, and oops, had killed his wife in the process.

Yeah. Right.

Knowing that she would have to tell him sooner or later, Abby admitted her cowardice in opting for later. Besides, she couldn't tell Houston about her suspicions of Gil. Not without proof. Which, unfortunately, she didn't have.

She had gone over the file again after talking to Brax. Nothing. Not one damned thing. She was beginning to hate the sight of that file. As it was, she could practically recite the thing from memory. But, most infuriating of all was that no matter how many times she read it, nothing jumped off the page and said, "Here's what you've been looking for." Nothing, absolutely nothing rang any bells.

Frustrated, Abby went to the kitchen for one of the sodas left behind from the abandoned pizza lunch, and popped the tab. The can was halfway to her mouth when it hit her.

Nothing rang any bells.

Bells. Bell...

"Bell," she whispered. "The ship's bell."

Abby practically tossed the full can of soda into the sink in her haste to get to the file. She dug through the endless stack of papers, searching for—

"There it is." She snatched up the copy of Houston's EUO. "I know it's in here. Where is it?" Furi-

ously licking her thumb to help her leaf through the
pages, she flipped through until she found what she was
looking for—what she had been looking for all along.
And it had been right under her nose. She found the
page, ran her finger over the words until she came to the
exact spot....

Daly: And you actually saw the boat sink?
Sinclair: Yes. Yes.
Daly: Afterward, did you see any debris, or Mrs.
Leland's body?
Sinclair: Yes, and—and no. I saw the ship's bell.
Or what was left of it.
Daly: The bell was floating?
Sinclair: No. It was still bolted to a piece of the
hull.
Daly: How large a piece?
Sinclair: Small. Maybe one by two feet.
Daly: You say a bell was attached to it?
Sinclair: Yes. Standard brass bell. Most ships have
them. It was engraved with the ship's name and the
date we went into business.
Daly: Did you consider picking up the piece of fi-
berglass, and putting it in the raft with you?
Sinclair: What?
Daly: Did you consider picking up—
Sinclair: You want to know why I didn't think
about collecting debris when I had just seen some-
one I cared about die?
Daly: I merely—
Sinclair: No. I didn't pick up the damn bell. How
the hell can you even ask such a question? Do you
know what horror is, Mr. Daly?

The ship's bell had still been afloat after the explosion. Astonished, Abby read the passage again. How

could she have missed this before? How could Gunderson and Brax have missed it?

She rummaged further through the file until she found the report regarding salvage yards that had been contacted during the initial investigation. None of them had found anything.

What if it sank? It could have. Minutes or hours after the explosion. Or it could have floated around for days, even weeks, then sunk.

But what if it didn't sink?

And if it didn't, what if, somehow, someone had picked it up?

Debris from a destroyed vessel didn't always turn up immediately. In fact, it wasn't out of the ordinary for debris to show up much later. Abby was a little surprised that a customary second check of salvage yards hadn't already been done. But according to the report, it hadn't.

That meant that there was a possibility—granted, a slim one—that the piece of fiberglass Houston had described to Daly was either still floating around out there in the Pacific, had washed up on a deserted beach somewhere, or was sitting in some salvage yard.

Just the thought of the last alternative sent excitement jumping through her body like water hopping on a hot griddle. All she needed was one tiny piece of that fiberglass in order to have it tested. One tiny piece, and the lab could analyze it for traces of explosives. One tiny piece, and she would know if the *Two of a Kind* had exploded accidentally. Or on purpose.

For a few euphoric moments, Abby could hardly contain her excitement. But then reality reared its ugly head, and her enthusiasm plummeted. What were the odds that she could find that piece of fiberglass with that particular bell still attached?

A million to one? A cajillion to one?

"Damn!" She felt frustrated, thwarted at every turn, and totally inadequate. She wanted to throw something; better yet, break something. At that moment the sound of breaking glass would have been enormously satisfying.

Abby pitched the file onto the desk none too gently, and sat down hard on the sofa. She yanked up a decorative pillow and whacked it three good licks against one of the cushions.

After a few moments of deep breathing, she was calmer. If Brax could see her like this, he would pull her off the case so fast it would make her dizzy. Her behavior was so un-Abby-like, he would know in an instant that something was wrong. She had to get hold of herself before she called him. If she could avoid talking to him again, she would, but he was her fastest source of information; or more accurately, the company computers were. They could spit out a list of salvage yards in less time than it would take for her to shower and get ready to go to dinner with Houston.

She glanced at her watch. It was early afternoon. Once she got the list, if she hustled, she could probably make a lot of phone calls. Experience had taught her that in this kind of work, personal contact often made the difference between being ignored and getting some very pertinent information.

No big deal, Abby thought, reaching for the phone to call Brax. After all, how long could the list be?

The list, she discovered an hour later, was three pages long. Two hours, two pages, and one very tender index finger later, she hit pay dirt.

A small salvage yard in Hilo had acquired a bell shortly after an explosion that loosely fit the description of the one involving the *Two of a Kind*.

"Yeah, we got one that pretty much sounds like the one you're looking for," Mr. Wallace, the manager of the yard told Abby. "If it's the one I'm thinking of, it was burned pretty bad. Think it got tossed in the resurrection pile."

"I beg your pardon?"

He laughed. "Aw, we get a lotta stuff that looks bad when it comes in, but if you clean it up real good, you can sell it. You know, sorta bring it back to life."

"Oh, I see. And you think that's where the bell is? In your resurrection stack?"

"Pile. Yeah, probably."

"Mr. Wallace, could you find it in that pile, and hold it until I can get there to look at it?"

"Depends."

"On what?"

"On how long it takes you to get here."

"I can be there tomorrow. That fast enough for you?"

"Yeah. I'll need a credit-card number to hold it."

"Certainly." Abby gave him a number. "And can you bring it back to life for me?"

"Extra charge for that."

"I understand. But if there's any engraving on the bell, I need to be able to read it."

"It's your money."

It was more than money, Abby thought, after ending her conversation with the salvage-yard manager. It could very well be a man's freedom.

She booked a flight to Hilo on the big island of Hawaii for seven the following morning, and a return flight for early afternoon. Then she took a shower and dressed in the caramel-colored linen sundress she had worn the first time Houston took her to dinner. Tonight she added the matching bolero jacket piped in crisp white.

Dressed for her date, Abby glanced around her bedroom, pausing to run down a mental checklist. She had her reservation. Her laptop computer and fax were tucked away in their respective cases, right beside her bag. She had everything she needed. She was all set, except for one small thing.

She had to tell Houston more lies.

She had to find some excuse not to see him tomorrow. An excuse he wouldn't question; wouldn't try to talk her out of.

She thought about telling him she had decided to go to Oahu for the day. But she might have a little trouble making him believe that she wanted to see Pearl Harbor and the Arizona Memorial more than she wanted to be with him. Especially since being away from Houston was the last thing she wanted. She was afraid he would see the lie in her eyes. And if he asked her not to go, what then?

Standing in the doorway, she stared at the three items ready for travel. It suddenly struck her that putting them in her bedroom so far in advance of her trip was a rather Freudian thing to do. As long as her bags were in here, she had to keep Houston out. Was this her way of making sure she didn't succumb to all that Sinclair charm? Her way of making certain the date ended with dinner and not breakfast?

But the idea of sharing breakfast with him was so appealing. Breakfast in bed. Warm croissants, and long, slow kisses. Hot coffee, and hotter passion. That was the way it would be. She knew it. Even now, just the thought of it made her body tingle. Making love to Houston would be like nothing she had ever experienced. It would change everything. It would change her.

Maybe that was why she had put the suitcase, computer and fax in her bedroom. An insurance policy against the natural disaster known as Houston Sinclair. Only, like most natural disasters, there was little to be done in the way of prevention. For the moment, the best she could do was try to stay out of its way.

"Stop it," she hissed, closing the bedroom door. "Just stop it right now."

That was when she realized she couldn't lie to him face-to-face. They couldn't be in the same room without touching each other. Today had proved that. And one touch was never enough. Not for her. Not for him.

Abby knew she was taking the coward's way out, but she didn't care. So long as she didn't have to be standing in Houston's arms and lying. Again. Quickly, so she could catch him before he drove in from the mountains, she dialed his number.

"Hello."

"Hello," she said softly.

"Abby?"

"I, uh… I hate to do this at the last minute, but…"

"Are you all right?"

"Actually, no." She kept her voice just above a whisper. "I've got the mother of all headaches. Probably a combination of heat, humidity and the pollen from all these gorgeous flowers. Whatever." She sighed. "My head feels like someone is working on it with a sledgehammer."

"Did you take something for it?"

"Hmm. About ten minutes ago, but it hasn't kicked in yet."

"Are you lying down?"

"Hmm."

"In bed?"

Abby's eyes widened, her throat suddenly dry. "Uh, on the couch."

"Oh." Now it was his turn to sigh.

"I'm sorry we have to cancel tonight."

"We can go to dinner anytime."

He sounded so disappointed, she felt low enough to go eyeball-to-eyeball with a snake. "I know, but…"

"What?"

"I'm just . . . really sorry, that's all."

"If it'll make you feel any better, we'll call it a post-ponement instead of a cancellation."

"Yes, it does make me feel better." After a long stretch of silence, she asked, "You won't starve, will you?"

"Hey, you're talking to a rugged individualist, here. I can open a can with the best of them."

"Oh, great. Now I really do feel guilty."

"Just feel better. I don't like to think of you in pain."

Dear Lord, if he was any nicer, she was going to cry. "I—I need a couple of hours of sleep to knock the edge off this headache, and I'll be fine."

"What about you? You've got to eat."

"I'll get something from the restaurant later."

"Promise?"

"Promise."

"Will I see you tomorrow?"

"I hope so. But probably not until late in the day. I'd planned to do some shopping for my mom, and pick up something for the girls I work with, you know...." Lies, lies, and more lies. Where would they all end? "Why don't I call you."

"I'll be waiting."

"Thanks for being so understanding."

"You're welcome, and Abby..."

"Yes?"

"If you need anything, call me, please."

"You're sweet—"

"No, I'm not. Right now, I'd like nothing better than to be snuggled up beside you on that couch."

"Oh."

He chuckled softly. "Sleep tight, lovely Abby. I'll see you tomorrow."

After they hung up, Abby sat for a long time, thinking about all the lies she had already told him. And the lies still left for her to tell before she had proof of his innocence, or of someone's guilt. And the more she thought about it, the more depressed she became.

Finally, she shook off the disturbing thoughts and went into the bedroom. She changed into a slip gown of beige silk that fell to mid-thigh, and a matching robe. She cinched the robe's sash belt, scooped up the abandoned novel, and went back to the sofa. Settling down for what she hoped was a bit of distraction, she opened the book . . . and found the flower Houston had picked from his garden and tucked behind her ear. The depression returned, and brought an old friend.

Tears.

Buckets of tears. Oceans of them. She didn't know if they were for herself. Or Houston. Or for the awful dilemma she had created. Maybe for all of that. And once the tears started, they threatened to go on forever. By the time she had finished crying, her eyes were red and puffy, and she really did want to go to sleep. At least, asleep, she could forget about what she was doing and what would happen when Houston learned the truth about her.

She must have slept for some time, and like the proverbial rock, because when the noise—a knock at her door—roused her, it was dark outside. Running a hand through her unruly hair, she staggered to the door.

"Who's is it?"

"Open up, Abby. It's me."

Some men might look ridiculous standing under a glaring porch light at ten o'clock at night, holding a carton of food in one hand, and a small stuffed whale in the other. Houston did not. He looked handsome and sweet and wonderful—all the attributes that softened Abby's heart and made it impossible for her not to invite him in.

He held up the carton. "Chicken soup. I figured it couldn't hurt. You didn't order anything, did you?"

She shook her head. "And that?" She pointed to the whale.

"Aid and comfort."

"Thanks," she said, accepting the soft plush toy.

He came in, walked across the room and set the soup on the table. Now without something to hold, he nervously stuffed his hands in his pockets. "I told myself I would bring you the food, see if you were all right, then leave."

"You didn't have to go to all this trouble."

"Yes, I did. How's the head?"

"Better." She clutched the stuffed whale, suddenly aware of how she was dressed, how she must look. "I must look a mess."

"Not to me."

She looked like a sleep-tousled angel. Her hair was sexily mussed, and the light from the lamp sitting on the end table behind her gave it a halo effect—all soft focus and gold. And was that robe and whatever was under it, silk? God, he wanted to find out. He wanted to untie that sash, push the robe off her shoulders and put his mouth on her throat, her breasts, her belly.

"Well, I, uh, guess I'd better get moving." Because if he stayed, he knew what was going to happen. He would take her in his arms and kiss her. And from there it would be a short trip to the bedroom. Not that he was patting himself on the back for seductive prowess, but when they were together, the tension was unbelievably intense; minute by minute, rocking somewhere between a steady sizzle and an explosive charge.

He called himself several very colorful and succinct names for even thinking about sex when she obviously wasn't feeling well. The puffiness around her eyes testified to that. But, he couldn't ignore the desire, the wanting. At times it was so powerful, he couldn't breathe. The best thing he could do for both of them was leave.

"Would you like to stay. . . for a few minutes?"

The proviso she had tacked onto the end of the sentence was like being handed a death-row pardon. He could stay. If he behaved himself. But he knew himself too well.

"I, uh, don't think I should."

"Oh. Well, thanks for the good deed anyway."

"Look, Abby." He ran a hand through his hair. "Don't misunderstand what I'm about to say. I came over here with the best of intentions, but seeing you like this, all. : ."

"All what?"

"All soft, and sexy and—" he shrugged "—and, well . . . tempting, dammit. If I stay, there's no telling what will happen. So, I. . .I'd just better go, that's all."

Abby had to smile. She had never seen him so ruffled, so uncomfortable. If he had been sitting down, he would have been squirming. And even so, he was still trying to be as honest with her as he could.

"Is this some of your technique?"

"My what?"

"You know, that up-front-and-honest business you told me about."

"Oh, that." Now he grinned. "Is it working?"

Like a charm, she wanted to say, but didn't. Couldn't, at least not now. "That's what I thought. You were just playing with me, all along, weren't you?"

Abruptly, the smile vanished from his face. And in a desperately calm gesture, he pulled the lapels of her robe together over her breasts. "Do you honestly think I'm playing with you?"

All humor fled. "No, of course not. I was teasing—"

"Because nothing could be further from the truth. I've never been as serious in my life. I've never been in..." He stopped, realizing he had fisted the silk in his hands. He let go, and gently smoothed the fabric, warm from her body heat, over the swell of her breasts, over her collarbone. "Abby, we've got something going on here. You feel it. Just like I do. And I take that very seriously."

Stunned at his reaction, Abby simply stared into his dark brown eyes.

"You know I want you. At this moment, I want you so much it's like white-hot iron in my gut. I can't deny that's a part of what I feel. But it's more than that. I didn't expect to feel the way I do. I... Oh, hell, I'm not saying any of this very well."

He was saying it well enough to make her heart break. Well enough to make her long to say to hell with the job, to hell with everything but him.

She reached up and touched his cheek. "Houston—"

"No." His hand covered hers. "Don't say anything now," he told her, fearing she would say, Forget it, no way, buster. "Think about it. And have dinner with me tomorrow night at my house?"

"Yes. To both."

Houston realized he had been holding his breath, and he let it out in a slow trickle. He turned her hand up and kissed her palm, then simply held it. "Thank you."

They stood like that for long moments, holding hands, holding out hope for their hearts' desires. Finally, Houston leaned down and kissed her cheek.

"That's as close as I can get and hang on to my self-control." He kissed her cheek again, then walked to the door. "Good night, my lovely, luscious, Abby."

And then he was gone.

Abby stood where he had left her, hating herself for the web of deception she had created. And loving Houston.

On the drive home, Houston thought about the words that had almost tumbled out of his mouth tonight. Specifically, the *L* word. He had almost said he had never been in love like this before. And it wouldn't have been a lie. Because now he truly knew he had never been in love before. Period. Whatever he might have felt for the only other girl he had even been serious about, paled in comparison to what he felt for Abby.

Funny, he thought, what strange little twists and turns life could take. If it hadn't been for his insecurities, he might have married— What was her name? Oh, yes. Connie. He might have married Connie, and never met Abby. He wondered if the episode with Connie ever crossed Gil's mind. Particularly since it had almost ended their friendship permanently.

Houston remembered the night, just days short of college graduation and the finalization of his and Gil's plans to start a charter business together, when Connie told him that Gil had tried to force himself on her.

Blind with pain and rage, Houston had taken Connie's word for it, even though Gil had insisted she was jealous of their friendship, and that he had never touched her. Nothing had been the same after that. Gil had moved to California and joined the San Francisco Police Department. The ironic thing was that several months later, Houston had found Connie with another man, and realized that Gil had been telling the truth all along. Eventually, he and Gil patched up their relationship, albeit long distance, since by then he had joined the navy.

But that episode had taught him a lesson he had never forgotten. And he had sworn to Gil, and to himself that he would never take anyone's word at face value if it was going to destroy their friendship. He had made that mistake once. He would never do it again.

But that wasn't a worry where Abby was concerned.

The weather in Hilo was muggy. An overcast sky predicted rain. But showers in the islands were rarely severe, and usually short in duration. Still, Abby glanced skyward, hoping a possible shower didn't mean a delay in returning to Maui. She had to be back by evening.

The salvage yard was small, but loaded. Abby had never seen so many odds and ends of once-upon-a-time-seagoing vessels in one place.

"Mr. Wallace?" she asked when a man wearing a captain's cap approached her.

"At your service. What can I do for you?"

"I called yesterday about a bell that you salvaged. You're holding it for me."

"Right, you are. Miz Douglass, right?"

"Yes."

"C'mon to the back. We couldn't get it as clean as we'd like, but we did get down to a speck of the engraving."

"Great."

"Can't tell much."

She followed him around the main building that she supposed was the office, to a shed at the back of the yard. There, sitting on a workbench was a slice of fiberglass with a bell attached.

Abby licked her lips. Her heart was beating double time, and her palms were actually sweaty. What if this turned out to be another bell? The wrong bell? What if this trip was nothing more than a wild-goose chase?

"See here." Mr. Wallace picked up the piece of debris and turned it so that she could see the section of the corroded bell that had been cleaned. Or he had attempted to clean, at least. "Like I said, not much to see. You got three clear letters. *I-N-D*. The fourth letter, the one before the *I,* is almost gone. Could be a *W.*"

"Or a *K?*"

"Yeah, could be. Can't be certain."

"Close enough," Abby said, feeling hopeful, really hopeful for the first time.

She paid Mr. Wallace to package the bell for shipment to a forensic lab in Honolulu, then addressed the package and took it to the nearest overnight express office. The lab would test the fiberglass for residue, using a gas chromatograph that gives a baseline graph for different elements, flammable liquids and explosive materials. The test results would prove conclusively whether the explosion was accidental—for example, caused by a fuel-line leak—or if it had been set intentionally, and if so, what was used to trigger the explosion.

After she made sure the package was on its way, she went back to the airport. There she called the lab and told them the bell was en route. Then she called Brax with an update and made the necessary notations to the file, using her computer. Now all she had to do was wait.

Chapter 11

From the moment her plane lifted off from the Hilo airport, Abby knew where she was going when the flight landed in Maui. She was going straight to the dive shop. She was going to see Houston. No changing clothes. No unpacking. Just straight to Houston. She couldn't wait to see him.

But when she arrived, he wasn't there.

Stuart Baker informed her that he had taken some extra tanks down to Wailea, but he should be back within the hour. Abby felt as if someone had just landed a direct punch to her midriff. Disappointed, she decided she might as well go on to the condo.

"Hey, there," Gil said, coming down a flight of stairs at the back of the shop. Two large manila envelopes were tucked under his arm. "Lookin' for Houston?"

"Stuart just told me that he went to Wailea."

"Yeah, but he should be back shortly. You can wait for him." He put the envelopes on the counter and poured himself a cup of coffee. "Want some?"

"No, thanks."

"So, you changed your mind, huh?"

"Changed my mind? About what?"

"About taking on my partner. You know, amour." He wiggled his eyebrows.

"Oh, well—"

"Hey, I think it's great. I'm all for romance."

"I wouldn't exactly call it a romance."

"Whatever you call it, I haven't seen Houston this happy since before the accident."

"He, uh, told me a little bit about that," Abby said, curious what Leland's reaction would be.

Gil arched an eyebrow. "Did he?" Then he shrugged. "Well, good. He's kept it all bottled up inside him ever since it happened. We've talked about it, of course, but even then, I've felt that he was holding back. You know, not talking about his real feelings."

"I think that's hard for Houston."

"Yeah. Even in high school he was never one to spill his guts."

"Can I change my mind about that cup of coffee?" Abby asked.

"You bet." Gil set down his own cup, poured another, and handed it to her.

"Thanks." She did want to see Houston, but she also wanted this opportunity to talk to Gil. What exactly she hoped to accomplish, she wasn't sure. But her instincts were telling her that Gil liked for everyone to think he was a what-you-see-is-what-you-get kind of guy, when, in fact, he wasn't. It seemed highly implausible that anyone could be as easygoing or as uncomplicated as he appeared to be, particularly after losing a wife only nine months ago.

"Did Houston mention his...hesitation about going back in the water after the explosion?"

Abby sipped her coffee, careful to avoid Gil's gaze. She didn't like the way he said the word "hesitation." He might as well have come right out and said "fear." For someone who was supposed to be Houston's nearest and dearest friend, he had a strange way of showing it.

"Yes," she replied, her gaze finally meeting his. "He did." Leland's face was taut, the lines around his mouth set grimly.

"Well, maybe I was wrong about the big guy sharing his feelings. Seems he's told you everything."

There was an unmistakable trace of resentment in his voice. Was it possible Gil was jealous of her relationship with Houston? The thought made the hair on the back of Abby's neck stand up.

"To be honest," he said on a deep sigh, "I'm really glad. I think he's held back from talking to me because of Shelley. He didn't want to keep bringing up what happened, you know. There's one thing I know for sure. He may not always like to show it, but Houston's got a big heart."

This time when he looked into her eyes, the hardness was gone, replaced by sincere concern. Abby was stunned at the transformation. Gil Leland was a lot of things, but uncomplicated wasn't one of them.

"Well—" he put down his cup and picked up the two manila envelopes "—I'd love to hang around and talk to a pretty woman all day, but I'd better get my rear in gear."

"I didn't mean to hold you up. Thanks for the coffee, and would you ask Houston to call me?"

"Ask him yourself." Gil pointed to the front window of the dive shop where she could see the blue T-Bird pulling in.

At the sight of Houston unfolding his long, lean body out of the sports car, Abby's stomach did a jitterbug. "Thanks," she said, without looking at Gil.

"No sweat."

She waited, her heart beating fast, as Houston entered the shop. Lord, but he looked good. His jeans were old and faded, with multiple holes. And tight. The sleeves had been cut out of the denim shirt he wore, leaving well-toned muscles to be admired. Abby did.

Houston couldn't believe his eyes. "Abby?"

"Hi."

"I was just wishing the day would hurry by so I could see you, and here you are." He was totally unprepared for the instant surge of desire the moment he saw her. Or the powerful urge to take her in his arms right here, right now, and kiss her the way he wanted to.

"Here I am."

His eyes skimmed up, then down, then back up to lock with hers. "Yeah, here you are," he repeated.

"I, uh, Gil told me I could wait." My God, the man was utterly gorgeous. The only way he could look any better was without clothes.

"Gil?"

"He's—" She glanced over her shoulder to find no one behind the counter. "He was here a minute ago."

As she turned her body, the motion drew her dress taut across her breasts, and Houston's blood pressure shot up. If he didn't touch her soon, kiss her soon, he feared his body might spontaneously combust. "Have you—" He cleared his throat. "Are you in a hurry?"

She shook her head, wishing they were someplace private. The urge to touch him was so powerful, she clasped her hands together to control it.

"Would you like to come upstairs to the office for a minute?"

"Upstairs?"

"Yeah."

"To your private office?"

"Absolutely." There was a hard edge of lust glinting in his dark brown eyes.

"Oh, I see."

"I sure hope so. Because if I don't kiss you in the next fifteen seconds, I'll go insane."

"Oh, well," she said breathlessly. "I, uh, wouldn't want to be responsible for the breakdown of your mental health."

"Thank God." Houston grabbed her by the hand and pulled her with him up the stairs. Once they were inside the office, he closed the door and hauled her into his arms.

"I've thought about this all day." He feasted on her mouth. "God, you taste good."

"So do you." She did her own feasting.

He wanted to go on tasting her. He wanted to hold her against him, feel her body melt into his. He wanted to shove everything off the desk not three feet away, and let the fire take them.

"I'm greedy," he admitted. "I want more." He drew back and looked into her eyes. "A lot more."

"So do I."

He closed his eyes briefly, and when he opened them again, the hard edge of lust she had seen glinting there before had softened to smoldering desire.

"Are we still on for dinner?"

"Yes," she said, knowing he was asking about more than dinner, knowing she was answering about much more. "Yes."

"Will you be ready by seven-thirty?"

"Seven."

He grinned, deliriously happy. Happier than he could remember being in a long, long time. "Care to try for six-thirty?"

Abby glanced at her watch. "It's five-thirty now."

"And?"

"I'd have to leave right now to make six-thirty."

He groaned, and buried his face against her neck. "Too high a price to pay."

She threaded her fingers through his hair, lifting his face for another kiss. He happily obliged. "The sooner I leave, the sooner we can be together," she promised.

"Yes, but—"

The telephone on the desk rang.

"Damn." Houston stared at the phone, trying to decide whether to answer it or not, finally giving in. "That's twice a telephone has interrupted us. I'm seriously thinking of disconnecting every one in my house before you come over tonight." He stomped to the desk and answered it.

"Lone Star Dive Shop. Gil? I don't know. Hold on a minute." He put his hand over the phone and looked at Abby. "Did Gil say where he was going?"

She shook her head.

"I'm not sure," he said to whoever was on the other end of the line. "Fine, I'll have him call you."

After he hung up, Houston scribbled a message and number for Gil. "Oh, damn." He pointed to a computer disk lying on the desk. "Gil told me this morning that he had an appointment with the CPA."

"Was the call urgent?"

"Naw, not really. He's gone to take the quarterly tax figures. He'll be back in an hour or so."

As soon as Houston mentioned CPA, Abby's mind began to turn and click like cogs in a wheel. One of those latent instincts that had helped her move up the career ladder picked this moment to stand and demand attention. Why would Gil be taking information to the CPA? Wasn't that usually a bookkeeper's job?

Despite her feelings for Houston, everything in her practically screamed that this was important. She *had* to ask the question. "So, Gil takes care of your bookkeeping?"

"Yeah." Houston returned to nuzzle her ear. He rested his hand at her neck, his thumb stroking the side of her throat. "He has a knack with numbers. Always has."

A knack with numbers.

Suddenly Abby experienced one of those moments of illumination that make everything crystal clear. The realization was enlightening, so hit-the-nail-on-the-head perfect, her heart rate jumped. She was right. She knew it.

"Hmm," Houston said against her skin. "It's nice to know my touch makes your heart beat faster."

"It, uh . . ." Her hands clutched his shoulders. "Yes, it does."

And if she was right, Houston was in for major pain, and disappointment. He was in for the loss of a friend. As far as trusting was concerned, he was going to have the rug jerked out from under him.

"How about we just forget about the time, and go straight to my house?"

Abby wanted to cry, scream, and stomp her feet. Houston had trusted Gil most of his life. This was unfair. She wanted to throw her arms around him and tell him how much she loved him, in the hope that it could, would make up for what she was now certain Gil had done to him.

In the end, she settled for putting her arms around his neck to pull him down for another kiss. A wave of fierce protectiveness washed over her. With her hand at the back of his head, she pressed him closer, urging him to deepen the kiss. She leaned into him, into the kiss, almost with desperation.

"Whoa," he said when they finally broke apart. "Hey, what's this?" Frowning, he reached out and collected a tear from her cheek. "Abby, what's wrong?"

"Nothing," she lied, trying to smile.

"Did I say something or do something—"

"No," she rushed to assure him. "No. You didn't do anything wrong."

"Then why are you crying?"

"I'm not...really. It's just that—" she wiped away another tear "—strong emotions do this to me."

"Strong emotions?"

"Yes," she whispered. "I have a lot of them where you're concerned."

Part of her heart soared with just that much truth. Another part was heavy, breaking for what she knew was ahead—for both of them.

"So, these are happy tears?"

Because she couldn't trust her voice with the lie, she simply nodded her head.

"All right. But I couldn't stand it if I made you cry." He kissed her mouth, softly, sweetly.

"You didn't. Honest."

"If you say so. You know, if I kiss you one more time, we won't make six-thirty."

She smiled. "I know."

"C'mon." He took her hand and led her to the door. "I'll walk you to your car."

Abby kept up her smiling front all the way downstairs, out of the shop, and to her car. She kept it up while Houston hugged her, kissed her on the cheek and helped her into her car. She even kept it up when he closed her car door, leaned in through her open window and told her he was counting the minutes until six-thirty. She kept it up until she drove out of sight.

Then she started to cry so hard she had trouble seeing the road.

"Damn Gil Leland." She swiped at her wet cheeks. "Damn him, damn him, damn him." Her anger stayed with her all the way back to the condo.

"That rotten little son of a bitch," she said, slamming the front door behind her.

It all made sense now. No wonder none of Gil's gambling debts were outstanding. Oh, they had been paid off, all right.

And he had used money out of the Lone Star Dive Shop bank account to do it.

Abby couldn't think of a name foul enough to call Gil Leland. If he had been standing in front of her at that very moment, she wasn't certain murder would have been an impossibility. He had been using company funds to cover his losses for no telling how long. Probably long enough that it was becoming harder and harder to juggle the books effectively. Long enough that he'd become desperate.

So he'd decided to blow his problems out of the water. Only he hadn't counted on two people being aboard.

It didn't matter that she was essentially dealing with supposition. It didn't matter that she still had no proof. The proof would come. Abby knew it the way she knew the sun would come up tomorrow. And when it did, she was certain Leland would be implicated right up to his neck.

So certain, she never once considered the possibility that Houston might not believe her.

While preparing for their evening, Houston kept telling himself that just because she had "a lot of strong emotions where he was concerned,'' didn't mean she was in love with him. Yesterday, that might not have been very important to him. Today it was.

Because today he had missed seeing her, missed being with her, missed her—more than he had ever thought it was possible to miss anyone.

Because today he had discovered that he was in love with her.

When love had happened, he couldn't say. And at first, the realization had shaken him like a bad aftershock. But then, the more he thought about it, the more he knew it was true, and real. And right. His love for Abby had settled comfortably around his heart as if it had always been there, waiting for her to claim it.

She had given him back something he had thought he'd lost nine months ago. Something he'd feared he had lost forever. She had given him back hope.

But how long would that hope last if she knew the secret he carried inside him? Would she still smile so sweetly? Kiss him so passionately? Everything in him told him they could have something incredibly special together. Everything in him told him she was the one.

And tonight would be the perfect time to tell her. He wanted to make love to her. Hot and fast. Slow and easy. For hours and hours. Days. In the sunlight. Under the stars. Exactly the way he had told her he would. But as much as his soul cried out to express his love, he couldn't. Telling her he loved her before he told her the truth was cruelly dishonest, and manipulative. He couldn't. Even if it meant he would never have her, never make love to her. Even if it meant losing her for good.

He had to tell her the truth.

He had to tell her he was a coward.

* * *

"Did I tell you how great you look this evening? Not that you don't look terrific all the time," Houston said as they raced along Highway 30 toward his house.

"Great save. And yes, you've told me twice. But I don't mind." She had selected her favorite outfit for tonight, wanting to look her best for him. What appeared to be a dress was actually a skirt and blouse. Made from a gauzy periwinkle blue fabric, the skirt swirled around her slender body when she walked. The blouse, made of the same fabric, was a halter style that buttoned down the front and didn't permit the wearing of a bra. The buttons had taken her an infuriatingly long time to fasten. Her fingers had never been so slow or clumsy.

Houston dared to take his eyes off the road long enough to feast on her beauty. That dress she was wearing was a cross between Marilyn Monroe sexy, and schoolteacher prim, with that row of little pearl buttons down the front. "You're a very beautiful woman."

His voice sounded so... *desperate* was the only word that came to mind. But it must be her imagination. She was probably projecting her own fears. Abby looked at his profile. There was something different about him tonight. She struggled for the right word, and found *sober*. That's it, she thought. Regardless of his light banter, underneath it all, he was wrestling with something weighty.

"Where were you when I was a gangly thirteen-year-old with freckles and braces?" Since he was obviously trying to keep his dark mood at bay, the least she could do was help.

"What happened to the freckles?"

"Most of them went away."

"Most?"

"I've still got a few... here, and there."

He whipped the T-Bird into his driveway, killed the motor, then walked around and opened her door. She stepped out, and right into his arms.

"Freckles, huh?"

"Yes."

"After dinner, I think I'll conduct my own little treasure hunt and find them." He kissed her hard, and fast.

"I'll draw you a map," she offered, more than a little breathless.

He slipped his arm around her waist, and they walked into the house.

Once again Abby was struck by the feeling of welcome, the instant she stepped inside. "I like your house."

"Thanks. I like you in it." Seeing her here, he suddenly realized he wanted her in his home on a permanent basis. Would that ever happen after tonight? He took her hand, gave it a little squeeze. "C'mon into the kitchen with me."

"Oh, so now I have to work for my supper?"

"I promise, no hard labor."

He opened the refrigerator and removed a large bowl of salad greens, which he set on the counter. He handed her a paring knife and two tomatoes. "It's either this or washing dishes."

"Quick, give me those tomatoes," Abby said.

They worked together pulling the rest of the meal together. Houston had prepared a shrimp-and-pasta dish ahead of time, and now removed it from the warming oven to place on the table. Abby carried her finished salad to the dining nook. He grabbed the bread and wine, and followed her.

"Would you rather eat outside, like last time?"

"No, this is fine."

Actually, it was wonderful. Candles flickered from so many spots throughout the room that they winked like starlight. Handel's *Water Music* was playing again, and the mood was soft, seductive.

They ate, and talked of things inconsequential. The urgency and tension that had characterized their time together that afternoon had melted away.

For Houston it was an opportunity to simply enjoy being with her—the sound of her voice, the way she tilted her head when she laughed, the way her eyes went all soft and misty when he complimented her.

For Abby it was a time to hold on to the sheer joy of loving him. A precious little time, she knew. For now, she didn't want to think of what tomorrow might bring. All she wanted was tonight. All she wanted was to love him.

When they finished she helped him clear the dishes, then they went into the living room. The lights were low, more candles were scattered around the room. Music still played, but the selection had changed to some old seventies ballads.

"Tell me, Mr. Sinclair. What's your opinion on dancing?"

"Why, Miss Abigail, are you asking me to dance?"

"As a matter of fact, yes. I'll even let you lead."

"How can I resist such a generous offer?" he said, sweeping her into his embrace. "But first, I've got something for you." He reached into his pocket and withdrew a small velvet-covered box.

"I bought this the day we went to Whaler's Village. I had intended to give it to you that night, but you weren't feeling well." He opened the box to reveal a delicate locket on a chain. Set in filigree, it was an oval-shaped disk of whalebone, scarcely larger than a dime, which held a tiny scrimshawed humpback whale.

"It's . . ." She reached out and tentatively ran the tip of her finger over the astonishingly detailed work. "Absolutely stunning." Abby glanced up at Houston. "But, you shouldn't have."

"Too late. Do you like it?"

"Oh, yes."

"That's all that counts." He removed the locket and set the box aside. "Turn around."

Abby turned, and a second later he fastened the chain around her neck. "There," he said, turning her back to face him. "Perfect. Just like the lady who wears it."

"I don't know about that, but this—" she fingered the locket "—is a wonderful gift. Thank you, Houston. I'll treasure it."

"You're very—" he kissed her cheek "—welcome. Now where were we? Ah, yes." He whisked her into his arms and back to the dance. "Hmm, you feel good."

"So do you."

She felt like heaven in his arms, and he wanted to hold on to the feeling. He tightened his embrace. "Wouldn't it be nice if we could freeze time, and just hang on to this moment forever?"

"Yes." To freeze time? It would be wonderful, she thought. Too bad it was only a dream.

"On second thought, maybe that's not such a good idea."

"Why?"

"Because then you'd miss my dip." Smiling into her eyes, he demonstrated by arching her over his arm in a very graceful dip.

"Wouldn't have missed it for the world."

He eased her upright again. The smiled faded. "I wouldn't have missed you for the world."

She traced the outline of his beard with her fingertip. "But you didn't miss me. I'm right here." *For how long?* was the question that was tearing her apart.

"I came close to missing you. It scares me to think how close."

"You're talking about the accident?"

"Yes."

"Don't think about it," Abby whispered. "We're here now. Together. That's enough."

He stopped dancing. "Is it? God, I hope so."

"It's enough for me. I don't want to think about the past tonight. You're lucky you don't remember that painful part of yours."

"I wish I didn't."

"But you said—"

"Abby..." He led her to the sofa and pulled her down beside him. "I wasn't completely honest when I told you I didn't remember the accident."

"What do you mean, 'completely'?"

"I don't remember the details because I don't want to remember."

"But that's not so unusual—"

He took both her hands in his. "Abby, listen to me. What I don't remember means nothing. It's what I do remember that brings the nightmares. The secret that I keep that eats away at my soul like acid. And I have to tell you."

"No," Abby said, suddenly fearful. What if he told her something that would affect the investigation? Although as a professional she needed to hear it, as a woman she didn't want to. The woman in her won. "I don't want to know. It doesn't make any difference what you remember or what you don't remember."

"Yes, it does."

"No, Houston—"

"Abby." He caged her face in his hands. "Sweet Abby. You have to know."

And he had to know what she would do when she heard all he had to say. He had to be able to look into her eyes and see for himself if he had lost her.

"I've kept it locked up inside me for so long. You have to trust me, Abby. It's the only way."

She placed her hands over his. "A-all right," she said, taking his hands to hold them.

"Shelley wanted to surprise Gil, so she decided to come along at the last minute. The weather was calm when we left Lahaina. Late in the afternoon the wind came up, and we drifted off course slightly before I realized it. I—I remember thinking the sunset was one of the most spectacular I'd ever seen. Shelley agreed."

His mouth twisted into a tight grin, his voice changed, and he seemed to be talking more to himself than to her. "Funny how little things take on so much importance. She had this thing—she called it a tradition—about going below at the end of the day to brew a pot of coffee." Beneath her hand, his curled into a hard fist. "If she hadn't been so hung up on that stupid tradition, she'd probably still be alive."

He blinked, his eyes darted to Abby's. "I didn't mean that. It wasn't stupid. Sh-she—"

"It's all right, sweetheart. You don't have to feel guilty about saying that. It's all right."

"I was correcting our course." He started up again, but his voice was shaky. "She was in the galley or on the stairs, I'm not sure which, and then . . ." He closed his eyes as if he could shut out the memories. "I heard a loud noise, and then, then I was in the water. The . . . The next thing I remember is Sh-Shelley calling for me t-to help her. I don't know where I was or where she was. The fire was everywhere. But she was calling me . . . calling me."

He opened his eyes and looked straight into hers. "All I remember is that I turned away. Abby, she called out for me to help her, and I turned away." His voice broke. "And sh-she died."

"That's not possible," Abby said, straight from her heart. "You couldn't do something like that."

Houston stared at her, a thousand emotions whirling inside him, not the least of which was a powerful, overwhelming, soul-deep love for this woman. She hadn't been shocked or repulsed. She hadn't looked at him like he was some kind of vermin. If he hadn't loved her deeply, completely, before this moment, he did now.

"I wish that were true, but I remember it. Because I was a coward, Shelley died."

"Coward? You're no more a coward than I am fearless." She shook her head determinedly. "No, Houston. Your memory must be jumbled, confused. You told me yourself that the pieces didn't always fit together. I don't know what happened out there that terrible night, but I do know that you would never have turned your back on someone in trouble. Especially someone you cared about."

"Abby, I appreciate your unqualified support, but—"

"Try to remember."

"What?"

"Try to remember. That's the only way you'll ever know for sure."

"But I can't. I've tried. God, don't you think I've tried? Hundreds of times. But I don't remember."

"Try again. Please."

It was the way she said please that gave him any hope of success. She wasn't asking to prove a point. She was asking for him. Begging for the chance to give him back his self-respect, his hope.

"Close your eyes." She put her hand on his shoulder, urging him to lean back on the sofa. "Let your mind drift back to that night. Think about the noise. What happened after the noise?''

He held her hand, and she could see the rapid eye movement behind his eyelids.

"The noise . . . and the water," he said softly.

"That's right. You were in the water—"

"No, no."

"But the explosion must have thrown you into the water."

"No," he whispered.

Then she realized he must be blocking his memories because they began with being in the water. And this was the beginning of his fear.

"Houston." She soothed her fingers over his brow. "After the noise you were under the water, weren't you? You almost drowned, didn't you? Didn't you?" she said a little more forcefully this time.

Suddenly he clutched her hand so tightly, her circulation was threatened. His eyes snapped open.

"Yes!" The word exploded out of him.

He shot forward, put his head in his hands. "Oh, God, the water. Couldn't get to the surface. No air. No air. My lungs, burning—"

He took a deep breath, much the way she imagined he had done when he finally made it to the surface that night.

"One hull was sinking, jacking the other hull up out of the water. It was bad. I knew it was bad. Had to get to Shelley," he said, his breathing hard.

"Waves kept pulling me back, tossing me around. Threw me into the ship. My leg. I cut my leg. Forget the pain. Forget everything but getting to Shelley."

Abby realized he had lapsed into the present tense. In his mind he was there. Reliving that god-awful night.

"Then I heard her. She must be topside. Sounds like a bell. She must be hanging on to the ship's bell. 'I'm coming Shel. Hang on!' Crawling along starboard side." There was a pause, then he went on. "Raft. Got to have the raft. Can't survive without it. Shelley? The blood. Running down my leg right into the sea. No good. We'd be shark bait. Got to have the raft. 'Hang on, Shel. Just hang on.' Get it. Get the raft. Throw it. Hold on with one hand, and toss it—stretch, stretch— lean back as far as you can. Throw it. Hard."

Abby's whole body slumped in relief. Now she understood why he thought he had turned his back on Shelley Leland.

"Houston—"

"Now, just head toward her voice. No, no. The water. Got to get back on board. 'Jump, Shelley. Jump!'"

"Houston—"

"No! Oh, no-o-o..."

She put her hands on his face, and turned it to her. "Houston, listen to me." Finally, he focused on her face, her voice.

"Abby?"

"Yes, sweetheart. It's me. You're here in your own house, with me. And you remembered."

"And it doesn't change anything."

"Yes, it does! Don't you understand? You aren't a coward. You climbed on board the ship to save Shelley."

"But I turned—"

"No. You didn't turn away from her. You threw a raft into the water. *Over your back.* The event got all twisted up in your memory, and you thought you had abandoned Shelley when she needed you. You didn't. You were trying desperately to save her."

He grabbed both her hands in his. "I tried to get to her, but I fell back into the sea."

"Yes." Tears gathered in her eyes.

"I told her to jump."

"Yes."

"Then...there was another explosion. The ship...sank. And I..." His eyes widened. "Abby, I tried to find her."

"Yes, yes." Tears streaming down her face, she threw her arms around him. "I'm sure you did. I know you did. You tried to save her, Houston. Don't you see? You're not a coward. You never were."

"Abby, Abby," he said against her neck. "I didn't want to remember because I was afraid to confirm my worst fears." He pulled back and looked into her eyes. "But you knew. Somehow you knew pushing me to dig up the memories was what I needed. Thank you, thank you." His kissed her mouth, her cheek, her forehead, then retraced his path.

"I love you," he said, just before he kissed her long and hard.

Chapter 12

"You . . . you—"

"I love you."

Abby shook her head. "You're just . . . It was a spur-of-the-moment thing to say, because you're grate-ful—"

"Grateful? God, yes, I'm grateful. But that had nothing to do with saying 'I love you.'"

"Houston—"

"I wanted to say it this afternoon, the minute I saw you. I wanted to scoop you up in my arms, whirl you around, smother you with kisses, and tell you that I am totally, hopelessly in love with you. But I stopped myself because I was afraid when you found out the truth—or what I thought was the truth—you wouldn't want anything to do with me. But you didn't pull back, Abby. You not only didn't pull back, you refused to accept my fear-twisted memories. You believed in me when I didn't even believe in myself."

She was so stunned by his declaration that she didn't know how to respond. Oh, she knew how she would like to respond. She would like nothing better than to do exactly what he had mentioned—fling herself into his arms, smother him with kisses, and tell him over and over how much she loved him; how much she would always love him. But she couldn't.

"Abby?"

"I—I'm overwhelmed. I never thought..."

"Neither did I, at first. Is it so hard to take? My loving you?"

"No. It's wonderful, only..."

"Only you're not sure how you feel. If you're worried that I'm waiting for you to say the same thing, don't be."

At her wide-eyed expression, he only smiled. "I've already figured out that a woman as wonderful as you couldn't run around loose without an attachment or two in her past. I think maybe you've been hurt before. And maybe it's hard for you to trust again. Am I right?"

"Yes."

"You don't have to tell me the details. It doesn't matter. What matters is that I love you. And I want you to trust me with your love."

She looked dazzlingly beautiful in the candlelight. Her hair appeared aflame, and her skin looked like ivory velvet. "Will you let me love you, Abby?" He leaned forward to sip from her lips. "Will you?"

She couldn't get her breath, and her whole body was tingling from just his slightest touch. If he kissed her, really kissed her, she would be lost. She should tell him, beg him to stop. She should have that much courage, considering the bravery he had just displayed. But she didn't.

She couldn't offer her love. Not now, not after he had bared his soul. In the end, when he learned who she

was, what she was, the pain would be more, not less if
she did. No, she couldn't speak of love. But she could
show it.

And she wanted this moment. This brief window in
time. Call it selfish. Call it cowardly, for it was certainly that and more. She wanted a piece of his love to
hold on to when he was gone. Unlike Houston's, her
reality wasn't a twisted memory. And when her reality
became his, she would still have this time.

She wanted this sweet taste of what their future could
have been if things were different. She wanted it de-
voutly, desperately. Because she knew it was all she
would ever have.

He slipped his arm around her, pulling her close.
Then he stroked her hair, her face, ever so gently, his
touch light as a moonbeam. "Abby?"

Her head fell back in a gesture of surrender. A small
thing, but it sent desire firestorming through his body.
"I'm not sure I . . ."

He let his hand coast down her neck and over her
shoulder. "Yes, you are."

She shivered, a sweet, fierce longing shimmering
through her. "You're right," she whispered. "I am."
With that, she lifted her head to his waiting lips.

His mouth moved over hers in a moist, deep, endless
kiss, rife with passion, longing, hope, and a thousand
sensations.

What seemed like hours later, he took his lips from
hers and stood, offering her his hand. She took it,
knowing that doing so meant there was no going back.
Nothing could stop them now.

He led her into his bedroom.

Abby barely had time to notice the deep rich mascu-
line colors. The only thing she saw was the beautiful
antique rosewood bed with its ornate headboard that
went almost to the ceiling.

"Was this your great-grandmother's, too?" she asked, then gasped as he skimmed his lips down her throat.

"Great-grandfather's. He bought it for their wedding night."

Houston was struck by the significance of what he had just said. This night was like none other he had ever experienced. Not just because of all that he had told her, but because of all he felt for her. Love—deep, powerful and binding.

Slowly, and with infinitely more skill than she had exhibited when she buttoned the blouse, he undid the row of tiny pearl buttons, one by one. And when he was finished, when there was nothing holding the blouse together but his willpower, he put his hands on her throat and slid them down, down, along the locket's chain into the valley between her breasts, and pushed the fabric aside. At the first touch of cool air on her bare breasts, Abby sighed.

"Silk. Your skin feels like warm silk." His fingers stroked, caressed, sculpted her fullness. "Incredibly soft."

Abby had never felt so treasured, so cherished. And she wanted to return the feeling tenfold. Reaching out, she ran her hand over his cheek, along the line of his beard, then down his neck to the first button on his shirt. "I want to touch you."

Houston's hands left her only long enough to finish what she started. In seconds, he was shirtless. And her blouse lay discarded on the rug beside his bed.

She ran her hands up his arms, over his shoulders. Hard muscles. Hot skin. She kissed a spot at the top of his shoulder, then scattered more kisses across his chest to the other shoulder. The taste of him seeped into her, intoxicating her.

His hands on her hips, he pressed her lower body to his. And slowly, seductively, moved against her. Again and again. Then his hands slid up over her back, pressing her torso to his. Bare breasts to bare chest as his mouth came back to hers in a breath-stealing kiss.

The dual sensations were electrifying. Abby moaned.

Houston deepened the kiss, his tongue stroking hers. While his tongue did wicked, wonderful things, he unfastened her skirt. It fell to the floor.

Abby roused herself enough to step out of the skirt. Then she hooked her thumbs into the lacy waistband of her bikini panties and pushed them down over her hips. They joined the rest of her discarded clothes.

He simply stared. That first day she came into the shop he had thought her body beautiful. How could he have made such an understatement? She was sleek, graceful. Stunning.

He shed the rest of his clothes, stepped closer, took her in his arms and kissed her long and hard, softly and tenderly. Then he leaned her back far enough to put his mouth on the swell of first one breast, then the other. Moonlight and starlight spilled over them like a shimmering silver veil.

Her hands slipped from his shoulders as if boneless. Her breath came out on a trembling sigh as he laved his tongue over and around her; treasuring the taste of her, savoring.

Wearing nothing but his gift, she was exquisite, he thought, as he laid her back on his bed. Exquisitely beautiful. Exclusively his. He was stunned by the stab of possessiveness. Never had he experienced the need to hold a woman close as he did with Abby. Not just physically, but emotionally. In every way. It was both frightening and exhilarating.

"I'm not sure there're enough hours in the night for me to kiss you, love you," he whispered against the softness of her tummy.

Languid, and helpless to do anything but respond to his mouth, his hands, she drifted on the sensations like lazy smoke from smoldering fires. She was aware only of wanting more, even as she drifted. She wanted to move closer to the fire, until the heat burned her. It was the heat, his heat, she sought. When he stretched out beside her, his body contacting hers almost from head to toe, she turned, lifting her leg over his. "Yes," she whispered. "Love me."

Moving his hand between their bodies, he stroked the silken skin of her inner thigh, then higher. Higher still, stoking, stroking. Her hips rotated slowly to the delicious demand. Seeking, wanting, until she gasped with that first, shattering, sweet release.

While she was limp with pleasure, he entered her, filled her. Her body bowed, taking him, begging for more. He gladly granted her silent request until they were giving, taking, soaring. In the end they were together, shimmering in their rapture like two stars glowing in the night.

It was still night when she woke, but hardly dark. Moonlight filled the room, casting shadows both harsh and gentle. Abby lay very still, listening to the night.

For a moment she could imagine herself in a fairyland filled with moonbeams and stardust. She could imagine herself staying forever in this magical place. With Houston. She smiled, remembering his tenderness, the way he made her feel so incredibly special. With a sigh of pure pleasure, she turned, intending to snuggle next to him.

And found him watching her.

"I hope that smile was for me," he said in a hushed voice.

"Hmm." She slipped an arm around his waist. "Definitely."

"What time is it?" Automatically, he reached for the small alarm clock on the bedside table. But Abby grabbed his hand.

"I don't want to know what time it is. I'm not ready for the night to be over."

Houston forgot about the clock and took her in his arms instead. "Your wish is my command. Besides, neither am I."

She hugged him tighter, her cheek resting in the hollow between his neck and shoulder. "My wish is that I could stay right here forever."

"Then stay with me. We'll hang on to the stars."

"Just like that?" What a wonderful dream, she thought, wishing it were that easy. "Just let everything go?"

"Last I looked, this was everything."

"It is," she whispered, her heart nearly breaking. "Right now, it is."

"And later?"

Later was reality, and she wasn't prepared to deal with reality now. She lifted her head and kissed him. "Later will have to wait."

This time when they came together it was swift, deep and torrid—their bodies eager for another taste of the fulfillment they had experienced earlier. The fire, still smoldering, took only a kiss to reignite. And they both went willingly into the blaze.

For the first time in her life Abby understood the phrase, "the cold light of day." Standing in her bare feet in Houston's kitchen with butter yellow morning sunshine streaming through the windows, she felt cold, bleak. Holding a cup of coffee in one hand, she fingered the locket Houston had given her, and thought about the night they had just spent together. A bit of heaven and hell. The heaven of being in his arms, of loving him, and being loved by him. The hell of knowing that today she had to face reality.

Behind her, she heard Houston come into the kitchen, and she turned to him, smiling. "You want some more coffee?"

He shook his head. "By the time I get you back to your condo and get to the shop, it'll be almost ten."

"I could call a taxi," she offered.

"Over my dead body."

"Just trying to help."

He came over and wrapped her in his arms. "You help just by standing there looking so gorgeous."

"You need glasses."

"I can see just fine, thank you, and what I see—" he kissed her soundly "—I like. But, I have to tell you something."

"What?"

"This dress. Specifically, these." His fingers played up, then down the line of pearl buttons. "Almost drove me insane last night. The next time you wear it, I'm not responsible for the safekeeping of one button. If they all get ripped off, that's the price you pay."

"I can live with that."

"Good." His mouth took hers in a soft, sweet kiss. "And, since I was preoccupied last night and didn't mention it, thank you."

"For what?"

"For helping me, pushing me to deal with all that stuff I had been trying so hard not to deal with."

"I wasn't sure I was doing the right thing."

"You did. For the first time since the accident, I can think about it and not feel guilty. I'm not sure about going back in the water again. That part doesn't feel as if it's changed.''

"Maybe it will, in time."

"Maybe. So," he said, smiling, "what's on your agenda for today?"

"Not much. I have to check on a few things, and—"

"Check on a few things?"

"To see if something I asked about at one of the galleries on Front Street has arrived. The lady told me to check back in a couple of days." As cover-ups went, it wasn't great. But it didn't have to be, as long as Houston bought it. And, thank heaven, he did.

"Well, since you're going to be in my neck of the woods, how about I buy you lunch? Say, around eleven-thirty at the Hard Rock Café?"

"I'd love too. I'll meet you there."

"Great. Then it's settled." He kissed her hard and quick. "Grab your shoes. We've got to go."

Twenty minutes later, when he kissed her again, this time it was goodbye. She had insisted he not see her to her door, but drop her off and go straight into work. Smiling, she waved as he and the T-Bird disappeared out of sight. Once he was gone, her smile faded and her spirits drooped. Last night had been an idyllic reprieve from reality, but it was time to face her responsibilities.

Inside the condo, Abby checked for messages or faxes and, finding none, headed for the shower. She was surprised that there had been nothing from Brax, but, at the same time, she was relieved. He knew as well as she did that the lab tests would take time. What he didn't know was that she was certain the evidence would show that the catamaran had been deliberately destroyed.

Now, all she had to do was link Leland to the torch, and they had him. But unless she had a miracle or two up her sleeve, she didn't have the vaguest idea how to make that happen. The man the Seattle police were holding had supposedly never seen the man who hired him. So they couldn't flash a photo of Leland for identification. The money had always been delivered by messenger service, which had been paid in cash, using a fictitious name. So how did the torch identify someone he had only heard and not seen?

Simple. By identifying the voice.

Abby could have kicked herself. Why hadn't she thought of this before?

She had to find some way to make a solid connection between Gil and the torch. If a tape of his voice would do the trick, then that's what she had to do. Abby checked the batteries in her microrecorder, and made sure she had a clean tape. This afternoon she would go to the dive shop and engage Leland in conversation in order to record his voice. She could overnight the tape to Seattle and, if she was lucky, the identification and the results of the lab tests would get back to her at about the same time. Then she would have Gil Leland right where she wanted him. Caught.

Of course, when she did, she would also have to tell Houston the truth.

That meant her time with him was running out. That meant that the best thing ever to come into her life was a couple of days, maybe less, from walking away. And she would be alone again.

She still had the choice of putting distance between herself and Houston. She could still . . .

Who was she kidding? She could no more stay away from him now than she could meet that shark face-to-face again. Houston was in her heart, in her soul. She would never be free of him. More accurately, free of his memory. Because that was all she would have of him when he found out who she was. And, as far as she could see, there was no way to nab Leland without

Houston learning the truth. Sooner or later, probably sooner, she would have to face his anger and pain. She would have to see the look of tenderness in his eyes turn to hate.

Her fingers touched the locket. She hadn't taken it off since he'd put it on her, and she didn't ever want to. Eventually, she would have to remove it, because the feel of it against her skin would be a painful reminder of what she had lost. Yes, eventually she would lock the gift away because the memory would be too hurtful to relive.

But she would never be able to lock away the love in her heart, or the pain of losing Houston.

With a battered but still-steady spirit, she got dressed and went into Lahaina to meet him for lunch. She knew time was slipping through her fingers. She had to make every moment count.

Lunch was a fun, noisy affair with lots of locals, as well as tourists, packed into the popular restaurant. Abby was determined to enjoy every minute of the time she had left with Houston. Which wasn't hard to do, since he seemed to know and be known by so many people that they were hardly left to themselves for more than a few minutes at a time. Several shop owners dropped by their table to say hello and exchange a bit of business talk. A couple of the hula teachers who performed the free hula show at Lahaina Center stopped by, and Houston was quick to introduce Abby as a "very special lady." When he did, he reached across the table to hold her hand. The young women got the message, and even teased Houston about giving his heart to a mainlander.

"They were right about one thing," he said when they had gone.

"What's that?"

"I have given my heart to a mainlander." Still holding her hand, he traced a finger over her knuckles and up her wrist. "Abby, your vacation can't last forever—"

"Houston—"

At that moment the two couples at the table next to them burst into laughter, and Abby thanked her lucky stars. The conversation was turning serious, and she didn't want that now. She cupped her hand to her ear. "What? I can't hear you very well."

He looked at her for a moment, as if trying to decide whether to pursue his train of thought. "Never mind," he said, raising his voice to be heard. "We'll talk about it later."

How many more times could she put him off? How long could she stall?

"I'd like to take you out to dinner tonight and show you off," he said when they left the café.

"Show me off? Next thing I know, you'll be beating your chest, saying, 'Me Tarzan, you Jane,'" she teased.

"Hey, I never claimed to be a man of the nineties. I just want to take you someplace nice. Not real fancy, just . . . nice."

"Okay. I suppose I can find something suitable for 'nice' in my closet."

He ran his hand down the side of her neck and over her shoulder. "But no more little buttons."

Abby shivered from the sensual electricity his touch unleashed. "You know, it's a good thing we're in public."

"You think so?"

"If we weren't, I'd be tempted to really kiss right now."

"So, give in to temptation."

He leaned down, and she met him halfway for a kiss that left no doubt in her mind what they would be doing if they weren't in public.

"I'll see you at eight," he said, reluctantly dragging himself away from her lips.

The "someplace nice" turned out to be the North Beach Grill at the Embassy Suites Resort. The restaurant was on the beach, and had a spectacular view of the ocean. Several saltwater aquariums, pools and gardens divided the space up into five cozy dining areas. While Houston ordered a full rack of baby back ribs, Abby settled on the scampi Provençale.

"You've got to taste this Killer Sourdough Bread," he insisted, reaching for one of the four wedges the waiter had brought to their table.

"Killer, huh?"

"No." He laughed. "That's the name."

"You're kidding?"

"Scout's honor. Here, try this."

Abby bit into the wedge of bread he offered, and had to admit, it was indeed "killer." "Oh, my gosh." She licked a crumb from the corner of her mouth. "That's incredible stuff."

"It's got four kinds of cheese and garlic. Lots of garlic."

She reached for her own slice. "I hope you're eating some in self-defense."

Grinning, he polished off the remains of the piece she had just taken a bite of, then wiped his mouth. "Does that mean I can expect to be kissed before the night's over?"

"You can't tell what might happen before the night's..." Abby's voice trailed off as she glanced over Houston's shoulder, and saw Gil Leland.

"What?" Houston whipped his head around to see what had caught her attention. Naturally, he waved Gil over to their table. As he made his way toward them, Abby thought she saw him weave once or twice, and guessed he had been drinking.

"Hey, how y'all doing?" Gil slapped his partner on the back.

"We're doing great. You remember Abby?"

"Yes, I do. And at the risk of ruffling my partner's feathers, may I say, Miss Douglass." He took her hand, lifted it to his lips for a kiss, and it was all Abby could do to keep from jerking it away. "You are a vision."

She gave him a weak smile. "Thank you." When he released her hand, she put it out of sight in her lap and used her napkin to wipe off the spot his mouth had touched. Her observation had been correct; he had been drinking. The worst part was, she knew Houston would invite him to join them, and he did.

"Well, maybe just for a drink," Gil said when Houston made the predicted offer. "Then I'll leave you two lovebirds alone." He signaled a waitress, and ordered a gin and tonic.

Abby didn't miss the tight edge around the word "lovebirds." Houston, on the other hand, seemed oblivious to the nuance. It took all of her self-control to sit across the table from this man and exchange pleasantries. In her opinion he was vile beyond belief. Fortunately, she could concentrate on eating her meal.

"So, Abby," Gil said, directing the conversation to her. "Have you been completely seduced by paradise yet?"

"It's hard to resist." She noticed he'd emphasized another word—so slightly one would have had to really be listening to catch it. It was no accident that the word this time was "seduced." Leland was no fool, and it certainly didn't take a genius to see that she and Hous-

ton were close. For all she knew, Houston could even
have confided his feelings for her to his best friend. The
thought made her skin crawl, but it was reasonable.
Leland didn't like her, no matter how much charm he
spread. Now she knew he was more than a little jealous
of his partner. For an instant she wished she had thrown
her recorder into her purse, but then decided Leland was
too far gone. His speech was slightly slurred.

"Yeah, Houston and I dreamed about living here
most of our lives. Right, slick?"

"Absolutely."

"Now we got us a sweet little setup going. Took us a
while, but we're finally sitting pretty."

Gil is, at least, Abby thought. He certainly had a
sweet setup. The question was, how long did he think he
could get away with dipping into company funds without drawing the attention of the CPA, much less his
partner? And if Gil had half the gambling problem she
thought he did, even if he had covered himself now with
the insurance money, it wouldn't be enough. Sooner or
later, he would get in over his head again. What then?
Back to juggling Lone Star's books? Eventually, he
would be discovered.

And no matter when or how that happened, Houston would be devastated.

Gil tossed down the last of his drink and stood.
"Guess I better make myself scarce. Y'all enjoy your
dinner. And partner, if I were you, I wouldn't waste my
time with dessert when you've got a dish like that for
company."

"Are you headed home?" Houston asked.

"You bet."

"Good. See you tomorrow."

"You bet." He tipped an invisible hat to Abby. "So
long, beautiful." With that, he turned and made his way
out of the restaurant.

"He's, uh—"

"In his cups? I believe that's the nautical term," Abby finished for him.

"That, and rude."

His assessment surprised her, softened her attitude about the encounter. "It's all right."

"No. It's not. That last remark about dessert was uncalled for. I would have said something to him at the moment, but he wouldn't remember it in the morning. Sometimes he's about as mature as that group of water babies that hang around the dock. I'll talk to him tomorrow. It won't happen again."

Smiling, she put her hand over his. "Thanks. I could get used to having you around all the time to defend my honor."

He looked into her eyes. "I could get used to having you around all the time, period."

She couldn't face the questions she knew he wanted to ask. Where did they go from here? What happened when her vacation was over? He had no way of knowing those questions were irrelevant. And there was only one way she knew to distract him from those questions.

"You know how to flatter a girl's ego."

"We aim to please, ma'am."

"I can certainly testify to that."

He looked at her and smiled. "Are you flirting with me?"

"Well . . ." Under the table she put her hand on his knee. "We could go back to your place and find out."

And find out he did. That night their lovemaking was wild and fierce. Their kisses sizzled and sparked. And when their bodies joined, it was as if a madness overcame Abby, and she in turn passed it on to him. There were no soft words and gentle caresses, only need. Des-

perate, burning need. Need they satisfied, then re-
created.

And in the morning Abby distracted him again. And
again. Leaving little time for talk.

Chapter 13

The moment of truth, Abby thought, her hand poised over the telephone. The lab results from the fiberglass and the bell should be available today. All she had to do was pick up the phone and call. One phone call, and she would know for sure if the explosion was deliberate or accidental.

One phone call, and it would all be over. Including her relationship with Houston.

She pulled her hand away. She couldn't do this. But if she didn't, someone else would. The investigation wouldn't end once it was determined that the boat had been deliberately exploded—as Abby felt certain would be the case. No, she had to do it.

Before she could lose her nerve, she picked up the phone and dialed. Fifteen minutes later she had her answer. Thirty minutes later, she had the printed report via fax.

The gas chromatograph test showed a small amount of nitrate as well as fuel oil like the kind used in galleys. And they had been able to verify that the bell attached to the fiberglass had indeed been engraved with the name *Two of a Kind,* along with a date.

There it was in black-and-white. Proof positive that the "accident" was no accident at all. This information alone was enough to ensure that a full-scale investigation, probably involving not only the insurance company but the local authorities as well, was imminent. She had what she needed, what she had come to Maui to find.

Cause. The explosion was caused by the nitrate and an incendiary device, probably activated by a timer.

Opportunity for cause. Gil Leland had all the opportunity in the world. He had the connections to hire a torch.

Origin of fire. The explosion had probably taken place in the galley, hence the fuel oil mixed with the explosive material.

Motive.

The one piece of the puzzle yet to be proved. But she knew who had the strongest motive.

She had enough. Abby had worked on cases with considerably less information and seen them solidify, once the district attorney's office and lawyers for the insurance company went to work.

So, her job was done. It wasn't up to her to prove Leland's guilt beyond a shadow of a doubt. With what she had gathered so far, the next step of the investigation would probably be Leland's arrest, and seizure of all company records. It wouldn't be long before the truth—all of the truth—came out.

And she wouldn't even need to get a recording of Leland's voice. The Maui district attorney's office would probably be glad to take over that task once Gil was in custody. She would be willing to bet money that his bail would be high, considering the possible risk of flight.

The phrase "willing to bet" echoed through her head. All of this was about money. Leland needed it to cover his debts. The torch needed it to do the job. The insurance company needed it back. But there wasn't enough money on earth to cover her need. She needed Houston. And after today she would need a new heart, because the one she had would be shattered.

Very carefully, she gathered up all of her notes, the file, the faxes, and stacked them together. Then she placed the printed report from the forensic lab on top of the pile.

Houston answered the phone when she called the dive shop.

"Hey. I didn't expect to hear from you until tonight."

"I—I ... I need to talk to you, Houston."

"Sure. What's up?"

"We need to talk. Privately, if that's possible."

"I think Stuart can cover for me for a while. Abby, are you okay? You sound ... strange."

"I'm fine, really." Undoubtedly the biggest lie she had told yet, but it was necessary.

"Would you like to go to my place?"

"No," she insisted. There were too many wonderful memories associated with his house. She didn't want to tarnish them.

"All right, then. I'll come to the condo."

"How ... how soon can you get here?"

"In twenty minutes, but Abby—"

"Please, Houston. This is difficult enough. I'll explain everything once you get here."

"All right. I'll be there as quick as I can," he said, and hung up.

While she waited, Abby tried to think of all the happy moments they had shared. She tried to hang on to the memories, draw strength from them. Time crawled by. She checked the stack of notes twice just to keep her hands from shaking. It didn't work.

She jumped at the knock on her door.

He came straight in, and took her in his arms. "You scared the hell out of me. What's wrong?"

Abby stood in his embrace, her soul crying out to respond, but she didn't. She couldn't.

She slipped out of his arms and walked over to the table. "Houston, please. I promised you I would explain everything, and I will. Only... only I need you to sit down." She gestured to the sofa. "And listen to what I have to say."

He did as she asked, but only because he didn't know what else to do without an explanation.

Abby knitted her fingers together and brought them to her lips for a moment, then lowered them and took a deep breath.

"To begin with, I didn't come to Maui on vacation. My employer sent me. I work for an investigations agency that specializes in insurance fraud."

She waited for him to absorb what she had just told him. And from the look in his eyes, he hadn't gotten it. "I came to Maui to investigate the accident that killed Shelley Leland, and almost killed you."

"I don't understand. The insurance company already investigated. It was declared an accident, and the claim was paid."

"Yes. It was declared an accident. Until a man confessed that he had been hired to blow up your boat."

"Hired?"

She nodded. "The kind of person we call a 'torch.'"

He was entirely too calm. Why didn't he shout, rage, do something? "This torch confessed so he would get a lesser charge on another crime. It happens all the time. The, uh, insurance company felt there might be a basis for a case of fraud, and my company was hired to investigate."

When he started to speak, she stopped him. "It would be better if I finished before you start asking questions." She took another deep breath and continued.

"We . . . I found the piece of fiberglass you described in your interview with Mr. Daly." When his eyes widened, she pointed to the stack of papers. "Everything from the original investigation is here. Your examination under oath. Leland's. And a lot more. What we didn't know was whether or not the explosion was accidental. Today—" she picked up the top piece of paper "—I received a report from the forensic lab that tested the fiberglass. That explosion was detonated by a timer. It was deliberately set, Houston." It was the most difficult thing she had ever done, but Abby struggled to keep her voice steady, and as emotionless as possible.

"In cases like these, the most important factor is motive. Usually, it's money. I believe that's the case here. And I believe I know what that motive is, or was." Oh, God, she had to do this. She had to. There was no turning back now.

"I believe the person with the strongest motive was Gil. I think his gambling debts got out of control, and he had to find a way to cover them. I think he took money out of the company—your company—to do it. And if you check the books, I think you'll see for yourself—"

Houston shot up from the sofa, his hands fisted. "Have you lost your mind?"

There was so much pain in his eyes—so much she could barely look at him. "No."

In desperation, he grabbed her by the shoulders. "Abby, tell me I'm having a bad dream. Tell me this is some kind of hideous mistake, but—"

"There's no mistake. That boat was blown up, and in the process Shelley Leland died, and you almost did. There's no mistake."

He blinked, stared at her, then she saw his jaw clench. Abruptly, he pushed her away from him. If she hadn't been standing only a few inches from the table, she would have fallen.

"You lied to me."

The bitterness in his voice ripped her soul. "Yes."

"Why?"

"I—I couldn't tell you who I was because at first we didn't know which one of you—"

"You thought *I* was responsible?"

"Houston, you don't understand. In an investigation, everyone is suspect."

"Now you think Gil did it?"

"Yes, I do." He turned away, almost as if he couldn't bear to look at her.

"You have to look at all of the evidence, Houston. By your own admission, he has a problem with gambling. It's an addiction, and addictions have to be fed. Where do you think he gets the money that he bets on horses and cards? You told me yourself he goes to Las Vegas several times a year. The money has to come from somewhere. Again, from your own mouth, he has always done the company's books. He has a knack with numbers. You said so, yourself. Have you ever asked to look at the books? Have you? Or have you always trusted Gil without any questions? You can check it out for yourself, Houston. He may be clever, but even a clever embezzler makes mistakes. Leaves notes in certain columns, marks unusual places—"

He whirled around to face her. "I have always trusted Gil. And I still do. You're lying. I don't know why you're lying, but you are. You're trying to make me believe a lie, turn against him. I did that once before, but not this time."

"What are you talking about?"

"Years ago, a woman tried to convince me that Gil was untrustworthy. I believed her, and it was a lie. It almost ended our friendship. I promised myself it would never happen again."

Abby stared at him, stunned. How could he deny the evidence? "So you choose not to believe me because of some misguided sense of loyalty?"

"Loyalty? You don't even know the meaning of the word. I thought I had found a woman I could trust. I thought I had found a woman I could love for the rest of my life." His eyes glinted with disgust. "I found nothing."

"I know I've hurt you."

"No. You didn't hurt me. You cut me up into little pieces and left me to bleed to death."

His words were like a whiplash to her heart. "I wish it could have been different. I wish we could have met under different circumstances."

"Why? Instead of getting paid to lie, you would have done it for free?"

She wanted to touch him, to make him see that she had very little choice in this. "Houston—"

"And was sleeping with me part of your job, Abby?"

She drew back as if he had struck her. In effect, he had. She had suffered a blow to her heart that would be a long time, if ever, healing. "No. I made love to you because I..." She knew he wouldn't believe her, but she had to say it. "I love you."

"You what? Love? You don't know what love is. And trust?" He laughed, but the sound was cold, humorless. "You aren't even familiar with the concept."

"You're right about one thing. I didn't know what love—real love—was until I met you."

"You still don't."

"Can we please just sit down, and talk about this? Maybe then—"

"Maybe then I'll believe you? Believe that my best friend, the man who sobbed at my bedside while I recuperated in the hospital, tried to kill me? That he *did* kill his own wife?"

The incredulity in his voice was devastatingly real. So real that Abby realized that for the moment, at least, he couldn't believe her.

"For what it's worth, I don't think Gil set out to kill anyone. Certainly not his wife."

"Just me."

"I think he only wanted to get rid of the boat for the insurance money. And I think he intended for the explosion to take place after the boat had docked and you were safely off. There was no way he could have known Shelley would decide to come along at the last minute. Or that you would stop to help that other boat in trouble."

"So, he's just an accidental killer?"

"If that makes you feel better, yes."

"You are insane. Go away, Abby."

"They'll only send someone to take my place. There will be a full-scale investigation, and the company's records will be subpoenaed. This isn't over, Houston. It won't be over until they have the person responsible in custody."

"Fine. At least someone else won't be biased against Gil. We got a clean bill of health from the insurance company. You even paid the claim, for God's sake.

Now you're here on the word of some hopped-up thief? Did this jerk say that Gil was the man who hired him?"

"Not exactly. I'm hoping he will be able to ID Leland's voice."

"You don't even have a positive identification to connect Gil to this . . . this torch, but you expect me to accept your word?"

"It's more than that. If you would look for yourself—"

"I see all I need to. I see that you've worked real hard to destroy a man's reputation. And you won't quit until you do."

"It's putting pieces of a puzzle together, and these pieces fit. It's my job, Houston, and I'm good at what I do. This time, I wish I wasn't—"

"Oh, you're good, all right. Good at lying. Good at manipulating, suckering me in. And I was worried about telling you I was a coward. Worried that I wasn't good enough for you. That's rich, isn't it? I can't believe I poured my guts out to you so you could use it against my best friend."

"He's not the man you think he is."

"Just like you aren't the woman I thought you were. I want you out of here," he said, his voice cold as ice. "Off this island and out of my life. Now."

Then he turned and walked out the door.

Abby stared at the door he hadn't even bothered to close. Empty. She had never felt so empty in her life.

Houston didn't realize how fast he was driving until he looked down at the speedometer and saw that he was doing eighty along Highway 30. He eased back on the accelerator. Wrapping himself around a light standard wouldn't prove anything except that he had no business behind the wheel of a car in his condition. His hands were shaking, and his body was covered in sweat.

He pulled off on a side road leading to Royal Kaana-pali Golf Courses and killed the T-Bird's engine.

The world had gone stark raving mad in the past hour. His world, at any rate.

Abby. The woman he loved. No, not anymore. The woman he had trusted. No. She couldn't be trusted. She had lied.

She wanted him to believe that Gil had hired some-one to blow up his own boat. Impossible. Gil couldn't do something like that. He wasn't capable. They had been friends almost their entire lives. There was no way he would ever believe his friend and partner had that kind of larceny in his heart.

Abby had to be wrong.

And there was only one way to prove it.

"Where's Gil?" Houston asked when he walked into the shop.

"Lonnie had some trouble with the boat trailer, and Gil went down to Kihei boat ramp to see if he could help, or at least haul the tourists back here."

"How long has he been gone?"

"Hour. Maybe hour and a half."

"Tell him I'm upstairs when he comes in."

Stuart eyed him curiously, but didn't ask questions. "Sure thing."

In the office, Houston went to the desk, opened it, and found the key to the file cabinet where the receiv-ables and payables ledgers were kept. He unlocked the cabinet, removed the ledgers, took them to the desk and opened them. Scanning a page or two, he found noth-ing out of the ordinary. Granted, he wasn't totally cer-tain what all of the little marks and symbols meant. Gil had his own system, and it had worked well for him all these years.

"Abby has to be wrong."

"Wrong about what?"

Houston looked up to find Gil standing in the doorway. "Come on in and take a seat. You're not going to believe what I have to tell you."

He proceeded to tell Gil about the torch's accusations, the piece of fiberglass that had been found and tested, and, of course, Abby's allegations that the motive behind the crime was Gil's gambling debts.

"Is she out of her mind?" Gil asked when Houston finished.

"Apparently."

"And you decided to go over the books to prove her wrong?"

"Something like that."

"So—" he pointed to the ledger "—go ahead. That way you won't have any doubts."

"I don't have any doubts."

"Don't you? You sure she hasn't made you even the least bit suspicious? Go ahead, take a good look. I don't want any doubts."

Houston looked at the man he had known almost all his life, then looked at the open ledger in front of him. "No." He slammed the book shut. "I don't have to. I trust you."

"Thanks, man. For a couple of seconds I thought you might have believed her. Just a little, anyway."

"Now you're the one who's out of your mind. I came straight to these books because I knew that was the one sure way to prove all of Abby's so-called evidence was worthless."

"Well," Gil said, exhaling a deep breath. "Of course, you're right. You know what this reminds me of, don't you?"

"Connie."

" You got it."

"I thought about that earlier."

"What was her last name, anyway?"

Houston grinned. "Beats me. All I remember is what a mess she made of our friendship."

"Six years." Gil rose from his chair and walked to the window. "You were pretty crazy about her," he said over his shoulder.

"And now I can't remember her last name."

It wouldn't be the same with Abby. Six years, sixty years from now, he would have no difficulty remembering her name, the way she smiled, laughed. The thought of her betrayal was like a laceration to his soul. He knew it would be a long time, if ever, before the pain of loving her and losing her stopped.

Gil heard the pain in his friend's voice. He walked over to the desk, perched himself on the corner. "Hey, slick. I'm sorry. I thought she might be the one for you."

"Yeah. So did I."

"Well, at least you know what she is now. And we've seen the last of her."

"Unfortunately, Abby was right about one thing. The information she's gathered is enough to warrant another investigation. That means they probably will subpoena our records. It's a waste of time, and money." He picked up one of the ledgers. "Because one look at these, and they'll know how far off base they are."

"Yeah," Gil said. "One look at those, and they'll know."

Abby knew there was no rush for her to leave Maui today. She had apprised Brax of the situation. He had been upset at first, telling her she should have waited to confront Houston, but finally, he relented. She could have spent another night and caught a flight out tomorrow morning, but she had decided not to wait. Why wait? There was nothing here for her. Why not get back to the world she had left? The one that didn't include Houston.

She would have to file an extensive report once she returned to the main office, but otherwise she had done all she could on Maui. Professionally, everything was in order.

Personally, everything was a mess.

Packed and ready to leave, she took one last look around the condo. She was glad she and Houston had never made love here. It was hard enough to leave as it was. At least that was one more memory she wouldn't have to deal with. One more piece of her heart she didn't have to leave behind. What heart? she thought. Hers was in tatters. Every beat felt as if it was pumping out her life force, draining her of hope.

"Aloha," she whispered to the empty rooms. Then she picked up her bags, walked out and closed the door behind her, wishing with all her tattered heart that she could as easily close the door on her pain.

As she drove south on Highway 30, headed for the road that would take her across the island to Kahului and the airport, she promised herself that she wouldn't look as she passed the turn-off to Houston's neighborhood. She promised herself she wouldn't cry.

She failed on both counts.

In a few short hours she would be on her way back to Los Angeles. Tomorrow would be business as usual.

Who was she kidding? Certainly not herself. Tomorrow wouldn't be business as usual, because she was done with business. The investigation business, anyway. She didn't know if the decision had come as she packed, or possibly after she'd talked to Brax. Maybe even as soon as while she watched Houston drive out of her life. Whenever it had happened, Abby knew the decision to leave was the right thing for her. If she had been concerned about having lost her edge before she started this case, there was no question now.

She was done. Through. Finished. All that remained was to turn in her resignation. Brax would go through the roof, but he'd get over it. Too bad she couldn't say the same for herself, Abby thought, as she pulled into the rental-car agency at the Kahului airport.

She had done her job. She had her ticket—and what was left of her heart. She was going home.

Houston decided to go home.

But when he got there, he realized it was a bad idea.

Everything reminded him of Abby. When he sat on the sofa, he remembered the night she had helped him deal with his guilt over Shelley's death. When he walked into the kitchen, he remembered seeing her kissed by the morning sun after an incredible night of lovemaking. And his bed. Lord, how was he ever going to sleep in that bed again without being tortured by memories of the two of them together? It was his house, but she lived there. She was in every room, every corner.

No, coming home was definitely a bad idea. But where did he go? Where could he go that he could out-run the memories of her? It didn't make any difference if he was in his home, at the shop, or on another planet. She was still with him. He hated what she had done, but, God help him, he still loved her.

Deciding he might as well try to be productive in his melancholy, he drove back to the dive shop. Maybe he and Gil could go to dinner and have a few drinks. Anything was better than being alone.

Stuart was behind the counter signing up customers for a dive the following day when Houston walked in the back door.

"Is Gil around?"

"Not sure. He went out for a while, then came back. I haven't seen him in about thirty minutes. If he's here, he's upstairs."

"You need any help?" Houston asked, since Stuart was the only employee in sight.

"Naw. Got it covered."

"Sing out if you need me."

In the office Houston sat down at the company's recently purchased computer and began to enter information for a data base he was creating. The computer system had been his idea, and since he was the most knowledgeable about both hardware and software, the entire project had become his baby. Entering the data was boring, but it had to be done. As distractions went, it wasn't much, but at least it would keep his mind off Abby.

About an hour later, Stuart stuck his head in the office door. "Closing time."

Houston pushed his chair back. "All right."

"You staying for a while?"

"Yeah."

"Okay, I'll set the alarm as I leave."

"Thanks. See you tomorrow."

"Not me, you won't. Tomorrow is Sunday."

"Oh , yeah." He had been so wrapped up in Abby, he had actually lost track of the days. "I forgot. See you Monday."

"See ya."

He stared at the empty doorway, wondering how he would keep track of the days now that Abby was gone. And the nights. Long nights. Lonely nights.

Just then, he heard Stuart talking to someone. Then he heard footsteps coming up the stairs.

"That you, Gil?"

"Uh, no, sir." A young native boy peeked around the door. "The guy going out the door said it was all right for me to come on up."

"Can I help you?"

"Mr. Leland?"

"No. Houston Sinclair, his partner."

"Oh, okay. I've got a delivery. Front Street Travel Agency."

"Sure." Houston motioned the boy in, stood, and reached for his billfold for a tip. Lone Star had worked out a mutually profitable relationship with the travel agency, and it wasn't unusual to receive several deliveries each day concerning tourists who wanted to book their dive before they ever left home.

"I'll take it. Thanks."

"No problem, Mr. Sinclair."

Houston gave him a couple of dollars, then escorted him downstairs, decoded the alarm, and let him out. He reset the alarm then went back upstairs. He was about to toss the envelope onto the desk when he noticed it felt heavier than the usual one or two pieces of paper containing arrival dates and confirmation numbers. There was something extra in the envelope, and he decided to open it. Inside was the customary paperwork.

And an airline ticket to Fiji in Gil's name.

Why would Gil be going to Fiji? he wondered, laying the ticket on the desk. He hadn't mentioned anything about it when they'd talked earlier that same afternoon. And why Fiji? He didn't ever remember Gil expressing an interest in visiting the island. Curious.

He heard the alarm being decoded. "Gil?" he called out. No response. "Gil, is that you?"

There was another lengthy pause before Gil said, "Yeah. It's me." A few seconds later he walked into the office. "What are you doing here?"

"Killing time, mostly. When did you decide to go to Fiji?"

"What?"

Houston picked up the ticket. "This came a little while ago."

Gil stuffed his hands in his pockets and shrugged. "Just thought we could pick up some business. I talked to a guy the other day about some junkets."

"We've never done junkets before."

"Lots of money, I hear. We could make a killing. Besides, I could use a few days off. You can handle the shop. Stuart and Lonnie can handle whatever's been booked, so, I figured, why not? Do a little business, spend a little down time with some Fiji ladies. Sounds like heaven to me."

"Suit yourself."

"I usually do."

Houston started to stuff the ticket back into the envelope, then stopped. He stared at the ticket, then shook his head, not wanting to believe what he saw.

"I don't understand." He looked into his friend's eyes. "This is a one-way ticket."

Chapter 14

"Just give me the damn ticket, Houston, and forget it."

"Forget what?"

Gil held out his hand. "The ticket, please."

Houston handed it to him. "You want to explain what's going on?" He didn't want to believe that this was all tied up with Abby and her investigation. He was trying hard not to believe it.

"I'm just taking a little trip. I told you."

"Cut the bull. This is me you're talking to. You're holding back, and I want to know the truth."

"The truth? You want the truth?" Gil shook his head. "No, slick. I don't think you do. I don't think you'd like the truth."

"What the hell does that mean?"

Gil was clearly becoming more agitated by the minute. Something was wrong. Drastically wrong.

"It means that you would be better off if you just let me walk out of here, no questions asked. Can you do that?"

"Gil, you're not making any sense," Houston said, when in fact, everything was beginning to make sense.

"You know—" Gil's hands curled into fists "—I was just going to disappear. Nice, clean. No muss. No fuss. But you had to... to..."

"To what?"

"Screw it up like you always do!" Gil shouted. "It's your fault that everything is messed up. I tried not to do it, but there's no other way."

"Gil."

"You had to go and crawl in bed with an insurance investigator, didn't you? My God, Houston, couldn't you tell she was stringing you along? She wasn't after you. She was after me. And you did everything but take her by the hand, didn't you?"

As he watched his friend change from easygoing to frantic practically before his eyes, the truth—the real truth—began to dawn on Houston. And Gil was right: he didn't like it.

And Abby was right. She had been right all along. He had refused to see the way she had pieced the puzzle together because he didn't want to see. Now, he had no choice.

"You did it, didn't you?" Houston said, straight out.

"I never set out to hurt anybody," Gil went on, ignoring the direct question. "I sure as hell never meant for anybody to get killed." He looked at Houston. "I loved Shelley. You know, after she was... Afterward, I started thinking that maybe that was my punishment. Can you beat that?" He started to pace. "I haven't been to confession in fifteen years, and all of a sudden I start thinking maybe I need to see a priest."

Houston watched the man he had known almost all his life unravel before his eyes. He didn't stop him. And he didn't walk away. They were both compelled to play this scene out to the end. No matter what the consequences.

"And when you didn't die, man, was I happy. A sign, you know. I took it as a sign that things would work out. Then she showed up, and ruined it all. I was going to fix it, you know. It just got out of hand. Everything just got out of hand. At first it was just a hundred dollars here, two hundred dollars there. But I hit a losing streak, and I couldn't break it. I knew sooner or later things would turn around, and I'd be on a roll again, but..."

"How much?" Houston asked calmly.

Gil stopped pacing. "What?"

"How much money did you take, Gil?"

"Uh, two hundred and twenty thousand. No, twenty-five. Yeah, that's it. Two hundred and twenty-five thousand."

"Why didn't you come to me? We could have found the money somewhere."

Gil laughed. "Don't you think I tried that? Couldn't get a loan. This wasn't exactly a sum you pull out of an automatic teller machine, you know. And the people I owed ... Well, let's just say they'll float you for only so long, then they aren't interested in excuses."

"But, to—"

"When they found you alive ... man, I was thrilled. I really was. You've got to believe me. I never meant to hurt you or ... I can't tell you what it did to me inside when I heard about Shelley. I swore right then and there that I would never gamble again."

"But you did."

"Yeah. You don't know what I've been going through since you told me about your lady investigator. I went over and over it in my mind until I just couldn't see any way out but to leave."

"Gil, listen to me. We can get you some help."

"Help? You mean jail, don't you? Maybe weekly visits to the prison psychologist? No, thanks. I was a cop, remember? I know what happens in those places," he said, his eyes wild. "Forget it. I'd kill myself first."

"Don't talk crazy." Gil was spiraling out of control. If Houston didn't do something to stop him, there was no telling what might happen.

"Crazy like a fox. You may have delayed my plans, but everything can still turn out for me. I just have to do a little readjusting, that's all."

"Gil, you're my friend, and if you won't take steps to help yourself, I'll do it for you." Houston picked up the phone.

"What are you doing?"

"I'm going to try and reach Abby at the airport. Maybe we can make a deal with the insurance company," he said, dialing. "If we make restitution, there's a possibility you can avoid prosecution."

"Hang up."

"It's the only—" Houston glanced up to find a gun in Gil's hand.

Abby sat at a small table in one of the airport coffee shops, an untouched soft drink in front of her. She should be checking in for her flight to Honolulu, but she couldn't bring herself to do it. Leaving Maui was breaking her final connection to Houston, and while her head told her it was necessary, her heart rebelled.

She closed her eyes, seeing again the pain in his eyes as she outlined her betrayal, step by step. She couldn't have done any more damage if she had taken a knife to his heart. And what had ever possessed her to think he would believe her in the first place? Gil Leland was like a brother to him. Why should he take her word at face value? She loved him, but it was too little, too late. He'd said that he loved her, and she had betrayed that love. He must hate her now. And she would have to live with that for the rest of her life.

But what kind of life would it be without him? A half life at best. Exactly the kind of life her mother had lived. Exactly the kind of life Abby had sworn she would avoid at all cost.

Memories, vividly painful memories, washed over her. The first time he kissed her. The night they had dinner in his garden and lay together in the hammock looking up at the stars. The wonderful drive through the mountains, and his own special place. Whaler's Village. All of it. Memories too painful to relive, too precious to forget. And in the end, what good were memories? They wouldn't keep her warm on a cold winter night. They couldn't ever replace the real thing.

Just then a voice announced her flight was boarding at gate fifteen. Abby heard the message repeated, and knew she had only minutes to check her bags and make the flight.

Only minutes to fly away from the only man she had ever truly loved.

Without a thought to the consequences, Abby jerked up her bags and started running. But instead of running toward the check-in counter, she ran toward the rental-car counter.

Houston was the best thing that had ever happened to her. And he loved her. What they had was too good to run away from. She had to go back and try to convince him that she loved him, would keep on loving him, no matter what. And if he rejected her, she wouldn't leave. Whether he believed her or not, there would be another investigation, and when Gil Leland was revealed for the scum he was, Houston was going to need a friend. Abby intended to be there for him. If that meant quitting her job and waiting tables just so she could stay in Maui, just so she could be near him, then so be it.

She rented a car and drove back across the island. More than once she had to caution herself to slow down. But she couldn't get to Houston fast enough to suit her. Anxious to see him, yet fearful he might reject her again, she thought about getting a hotel room, then calling him. But, as she approached the turnoff to his house, she couldn't resist.

But he wasn't home. Disappointed, she drove on into Lahaina.

It was almost dusk, and the harbor lights were beginning to flicker on. The streets were crowded with tourists and shoppers. The restaurant parking lots were full.

Abby knew the dive shop would be closed, but she also knew Houston and Gil often worked in the office after closing. Oh, Lord, she thought, what if she ran into Gil? No, she decided. Gil, or no Gil she had to find Houston.

When she pulled into a parking space across the street from the dive shop, she saw the T-Bird parked out front. She glanced up and saw the office light was on. He was here! Oh, thank God.

But would he listen to her? Would he even talk to her?

Abby made her way around to the back door, and was surprised to find Gil's old Jeep parked in the alley. Were they both upstairs? She knocked on the door and waited. And waited. No answer. She knocked again. Still no answer.

Since none of the office windows overlooked the alley, Abby was certain they didn't know who was knocking. So that eliminated the possibility that they knew it was her and simply refused to answer. The obvious possibility was that they weren't there. But both cars were. Suddenly the hair stood up on the back of her neck, and she couldn't shake the feeling that something was wrong.

Of course, Abby calmed herself, they could have walked to a nearby bar or restaurant. If that was the case, she stood little chance of finding Houston tonight. But she wanted to find him tonight. She needed to find him.

Feeling frustrated and dejected, she walked back to her car. What choice did she have but to find a room and wait until morning? For several moments she sat in her rented sedan, trying to decide her course of action. And in the back of her mind was the nagging feeling that something was wrong. She looked down toward the docks, at the boats in their slips, some rigged with lights. She looked again, harder this time.

There were lights on the Lone Star catamaran! She was sure of it. But Houston wouldn't be on the docks. If someone was aboard, it was Gil.

Abby thought about it for a long time, then decided that if the only way she could find Houston tonight was to confront Gil, then that's the way it would have to be. She locked her car and walked toward the docks. As she neared the boat, she noticed lights were on below, but saw no one on deck. Gil must be below. Stopping at the edge of the narrow gangplank, Abby glanced at the catamaran gently rising and falling as a slight wind whipped through the harbor. Then she glanced down at the water. So dark. So deep. Fear, cold and clammy, seized her and for a moment she felt dizzy.

She could do this. She had to do this. But not in these shoes, she thought, slipping off her two-inch pumps and stuffing them into the pocket of her blazer. She would have preferred shorts instead of the long gauzy skirt that whipped around her legs in the wind, but she would just have to make the best of it. Holding onto the rail, she carefully made her way across the gangplank, onto the deck. She took a deep, steadying breath... and realized there were voices coming from below deck. And both voices were male.

There were a dozen possibilities of who the second man could be, but instinctively Abby knew it was Houston. Gathering a handful of her flyaway skirt in one hand, she made her way across the swaying hull, to the cabin situated between the twin hulls. The roof of the cabin rose a good four feet above the deck, and the hatch cover was open to the steps leading to the galley and wheelhouse.

But she stopped short of the first step when she heard Gil speak.

"I wish there was another way to do this, Houston. But there's just not. I have to get those people off my back for good. One more time—won't you let me walk away? All you have to do is keep your mouth shut."

"I can't. You've stolen. Hell, you've killed, and I can't let you walk away. But I'm asking you, begging you, not to do this, Gil."

"Sorry. I'm out of options, slick."

"Killing me isn't the answer. And no one is going to believe a suicide."

Abby's heart shot into her throat. He was going to kill Houston! She bent down, edging closer.

"Why not? Lots of people around here know you felt guilty about Shelley's death. Lots of people know how depressed you've been. And it's fitting that you would decide to end your life the same way Shelley died."

"No one will believe it."

"I'll leave a little note on your computer that will help convince everyone. By the time the police find it, I'll be long gone."

"To spend the rest of your life running, hiding? What kind of life is that, Gil?"

"I told you. Anything is better than prison. Now, shut up."

Someone was coming up the steps! Quickly, Abby crept around to the back side of the cabin and flattened herself against the deck. Aided by the cover of darkness, she peeked around the corner of the cabin and saw Gil walk forward, cast off, then walk back down below deck. If he felt free to leave Houston below, that must mean Houston wasn't free, Abby surmised. Gil must have him tied up or somehow confined.

Suddenly the engine jumped to life, and Abby started to roll. Her hand shot up to grasp the hatch cover as the boat moved out of its slip and out into the harbor. If the boat was moving, Gil was obviously at the wheel; and if he was at the wheel, he didn't have a clear view of the cabin stairs. Without any thought about what might happen to her, Abby crept back around the cabin and down the steps.

The instant he saw her, Houston opened his mouth to call her name, but she put her finger to her lips in warning. His hands were tied, and the rope stretched down around the leg of the bench-style table that was bolted to the deck. Abby slipped into the opening to the glass-bottom pontoon closest to Houston.

"For God's sake, Abby, get off this boat," Houston whispered, keeping his eyes straight ahead. "He's got a gun."

"Not without you," she whispered back.

"You see that box over there?" With a nod of his head he gestured to a copy-paper box sitting atop a counter used to serve snacks to customers. "He's got explosives and a timer in there. You've got to get off. Now!"

"No."

They were moving out of the harbor and soon they would be headed out to sea. There was no time to argue with her, Houston decided. "In my pocket is a penknife," he said, praying the small blade was sharp enough to cut through the rope. "Can you get it?"

"I'll try." Abby crawled out of the opening and scooted under the table directly behind Houston's legs. "Which pocket?"

"Right." He shifted his body and leaned back as far as he could.

Abby reached up and tried to work her hand into his jeans pocket, but the denim was tight. Finally, she settled for wiggling her fingers far enough down to maneuver the knife up and out. "Got it!" She flipped the blade out and started sawing at the rope. Working furiously, she felt the seconds tick by like hours while she worked. At last, the rope popped in two. She pulled and tugged until at last Houston was free.

He spun around, reaching under the table for Abby at the same time, jerked her up and half dragged, half carried her to the steps leading above deck.

"Houston!"

He whipped around to see Gil standing by the wheelhouse, his gun pointed at both of them. He saw Gil's other hand come up in the customary policeman's hold and reacted instinctively.

Gil fired at the same moment Houston shoved Abby to one side.

Abby screamed, falling onto the deck. A second later, Houston's body fell on hers.

"I'm all right. Crawl. To the back of the boat."

Another bullet whizzed over their heads.

"Keep going. There's a ladder that goes to the upper deck."

With Houston acting as a shield, they scrambled to the ladder just as Gil rounded the serving counter, aimed and fired.

Abby thought she heard Houston moan but she wasn't sure, and he stayed right behind her going up the ladder. They were on deck, but far from safe. Gil was still below with the explosives and a gun.

"He's got a dinghy lashed to the left hull so he can get back to the docks." Houston grabbed her hand and pulled her along the side of the cabin, heading for the rowboat. Her hand slipped out of his and she looked down as he reached for it again.

Houston's arm and both of their hands were covered in blood.

"Oh, my God," she cried. "You're hurt."

"Keep moving."

"But you're—"

"It doesn't matter now—"

"Stop right where you are!" Gil called from behind them.

They stopped, turned to face him, and Houston pushed Abby behind him.

They stood on one side of the cabin's entrance, Gil on the other, an equal distance from the dinghy.

"Didn't think I'd let you get away, did you?"

"You're not a killer, Gil. It's not too late to put a stop to this. Give it up." Reaching a hand behind him to urge Abby to stay with him, Houston inched his way toward Gil.

"Stay right where you are," Gil ordered when they were less than three feet from him. "You're up to something."

Houston shook his head. "I want to see your face. I want you to look me in the eye when you shoot me."

"Oh, no." Gil grinned. "I couldn't kill you out-right. The explosives will do that. Neat, huh?"

Houston's hopes of getting Abby to the dinghy and safety suddenly nosedived. Unless he could get that gun away from Gil, their chances of survival were slim to none.

"Now," Gil said, backing up, "I'm going to get in my little boat, paddle out a way and wait for the big boom." He glanced down to check his path.

Houston saw his opportunity and took it.

He leaped forward, grabbed for the gun and he and Gil went down in a tangle of limbs. They rolled around on the deck, struggling with the weapon, finally rolling through the cabin entrance and down the steps. Now they grappled on their knees for the pistol.

"Abby!" Houston yelled. "Get to the dinghy. Hurry!"

The pitch and sway of the boat sent them tumbling over the deck and up against the right pontoon. The gun popped free and went sliding across the deck. Both men shot to their feet, trying to prevent the other from reaching the weapon. As they staggered backward together, Gil took a swing at Houston and missed. Houston's fist caught Gil square on the jaw, slamming him against the serving counter.

In one swift move, Gil righted himself and grabbed Houston, knocking the box of explosives and timer to the deck in the process. Neither man noticed. All their attention was focused on seizing the gun. They both dove for it, but at that moment the boat pitched, and the weapon skidded across the deck and fell down into the open glass-bottom area.

As Gil watched the pistol disappear out of sight, Houston hit him with a powerful blow to the right side of his head. Gil groaned, then slumped onto the deck. Houston grabbed his friend by the back of the shirt and dragged him up the stairs. He was almost in the open, hanging on to Gil, when the explosion ripped through the cabin, jerking Gil from his grasp and hurling him several feet along the upper deck.

Houston looked up in time to see Abby fly over the ship's railing and plunge into the ocean.

"Abby! Abby!" Dragging himself to the railing he scanned the waves for her. Finally he saw her floating, facedown, in the water.

Houston dove straight for her, but when he surfaced, he couldn't see her. "No. Not again. Do you hear me?" he yelled. He prayed. "Not again."

Just then, another explosion lit up the darkness. "Abby!" he screamed, twisting and turning, searching.... Then he saw her—saw something about twenty yards away. Keeping his eyes fixed on the spot, he swam furiously toward it. But just before he reached the spot, she disappeared beneath the waves.

Houston dived, frantically groping for her in the inky water. Then something that felt like seaweed brushed his hand and he grabbed at it.

And found he had a handful of Abby's skirt.

He yanked the sodden fabric toward him and pulled her limp body into his arms. With three powerful kicks, they broke the surface of the water.

"Abby, Abby." He held her head in his hands, shaking it gently. "Talk to me. Sweetheart. Oh, God, don't let her be—"

She made a choking sound, coughing up seawater, and Houston thought it just might be the most beautiful sound in the world. He turned her, looping her arms around his neck. "Hang on, sweetheart."

"Hou-Houston," Abby finally managed to choke out his name.

"It's okay. I'm here. You're safe."

Still coughing, she looked up and saw that a great deal of the boat was now on fire. "Gil?"

"He's still on board."

Suddenly a screaming apparition appeared on the deck of the burning ship. It was Gil, most of his body engulfed in flames. For a second he paused, arms outstretched like some monster in a horror movie. Then a second explosion ripped through the night, destroying the ship completely. And he was gone.

Chapter 15

"Are you warm enough?"

"Hmm." Sitting on the sofa wearing one of Houston's soft denim shirts and a pair of his boxer shorts pinned at the waist, Abby snuggled deeper under the quilt he had brought from his bedroom.

"More coffee? It's decaf."

Abby had to smile. It would take more than caffeine to keep her awake. After tonight's ordeal, she was so totally exhausted she just might sleep for days. "No, thanks."

They had managed to pull themselves into the dinghy and start rowing back toward the harbor, but they didn't have to row for very long. The explosion had been seen from the docks, and within moments the harbor-patrol boat and several others were on the scene to help. Wet, frightened and almost in shock, they had been questioned, signed statements, and in general, repeated the events of the night more times than either of them cared to remember.

Through all the questions, Houston had never left her side. They had huddled together under blankets for warmth, and sipped hot coffee together in a quiet corner while their statements were being typed. Now, alone in his house, for the first time Abby felt uncomfortable in his presence.

She looked so small and fragile, Houston thought. Small wonder, after what she had been through. It was almost ironic that he had once envisioned her sitting on this couch, wearing one of his shirts; and now here she was, but how different the circumstances. He wondered if he would ever have the opportunity to see the other fantasy fulfilled, or if she'd had enough of islands, the ocean, and him.

"I hung your clothes up in the kitchen, but I'm afraid the blazer is ruined," he said apologetically.

She reached up and brushed a still-damp swath of hair out of her eyes. "A small price to pay for my life, don't you think?"

Wearing nothing but a pair of jeans and a worried look on his face, Houston squatted in front of her, balancing himself on the balls of his feet. "You can't put a price on your life."

"Gil did. What was the amount? Two hundred and twenty-five thousand dollars?"

"I'd gladly give a hundred times that sum for you not to have gone through what you did tonight. Abby." He rocked forward, coming down on one knee. "If anything had happened to you..." He closed his eyes, whispering, "When I saw you going over the rail and into the water—" opening his eyes, he swallowed hard "—my heart stopped."

Abby thought she was all cried out, thought she had shaken until there wasn't one more tremble left in her body, but she was wrong. Seeing Houston so humble, so... frightened for her, brought the emotions whirling to the surface in a heartbeat. A fat teardrop slid down her cheek and plopped onto the quilt.

"Oh, darlin', no." Quickly, he was beside her, wrapping her in his embrace. "Don't cry, sweetheart. Please, don't cry."

But she couldn't stop. The tears she had shed before were out of fear, and from having to tell and retell the horror of what had happened. They had been necessary, but not cleansing. The tears she shed now, with Houston rocking her gently, washed her soul, cleansed her heart.

"Abby, Abby," he murmured against her temple. "I was a fool. Can you ever forgive me?".

"I—I lied," she sobbed.

"Don't." He held her tighter. "You did what you had to. I understand that now. And my reaction was so...so brutal. I'll never forgive myself."

"B-but Gil was y-your friend. You tr-trusted him. I sh-should have known you would be-be loyal. No matter w-what."

"I was blind, and it was almost too late by the time I really opened my eyes. I almost lost you."

"But you didn't. You saved me."

"No. When I dived in the water after you, I saved myself. I love you, Abby. I'm nothing without you."

She pulled a hand from beneath the quilt to stroke his cheek. "And I love you. I didn't think I would ever get the chance to say those words again."

"And now?"

"Now, I want to say them until you're sick of hearing them."

He smiled, kissed her damp cheek. "That should be in about fifty or sixty years."

"I was thinking more along the lines of forever."

Houston looked into her beautiful blue eyes and saw forgiveness, and more love than he deserved. "I like your time frame better."

"But..."

"But what? There's nothing we can't handle as long as we're together."

"What about...my job?"

He turned her to face him, lifting her arms around his neck. "You mean the investigation?" She nodded.

"I thought about that while we were standing around waiting for stenographers, for all the paperwork to be done." Absently, he massaged her shoulders. "I want to leave Maui, Abby."

"But—"

"No." He silenced her with a quick kiss. "Maybe I'll come back—we'll come back—someday as tourists, but this part of my life is over. I think it's been over for a while, and I didn't realize it until you came along. I want to go home, Abby. To Houston."

He waited, watching her face for any signs of distress, releasing a deep sigh when he found none. "Do you think you could be happy in Texas?"

"No more water, huh?"

"Actually, I was thinking of a marina along the coast. Maybe Padre Island."

"Another island?" she said, smiling.

"We don't have to," he rushed to assure her. "If you don't ever want to see the ocean again, I can live with that."

"You love the sea, and I love you. A marina sounds fine to me."

"But your job."

"I'm looking for a new job," she told him, caressing his broad shoulders. "Something less adventuresome."

"How does raising a couple of kids sound to you?"

Her hands stilled. "Kids?"

"Yeah. Marriage, kids. The works."

Abby smiled, her eyes shining with love as she drew his head down for a deep kiss. "It sounds like paradise."

*   *   *   *   *

FORTUNE'S Children™

In July, get to know the Fortune family....

Next month, don't miss the start of Fortune's Children, a
fabulous new twelve-book series from Silhouette Books.

**Meet the Fortunes—a family whose legacy is greater than
riches. Because where there's a will...there's a wedding!**

When Kate Fortune's plane crashes in the jungle, her family
believes that she's dead. And when her will is read, they
discover that Kate's plans for their lives are more interesting
than they'd ever suspected.

Look for the first book, *Hired Husband*, by *New York Times*
bestselling author **Rebecca Brandewyne**. PLUS, a stunning,
perforated bookmark is affixed to *Hired Husband* (and
selected other titles in the series), providing a convenient
checklist for all twelve titles!

FREE
Keepsake
Bookmark

Launching in July wherever books are sold.

This July, watch for the delivery of...

An exciting new miniseries that appears in a different Silhouette series each month. It's about love, marriage—and Daddy's unexpected need for a baby carriage!

Daddy Knows Last unites five of your favorite authors as they weave five connected stories about baby fever in New Hope, Texas.

- **THE BABY NOTION** by Dixie Browning
  (SD#1011, 7/96)

- **BABY IN A BASKET** by Helen R. Myers
  (SR#1169, 8/96)

- **MARRIED...WITH TWINS!**
  by Jennifer Mikels
  (SSE#1054, 9/96)

- **HOW TO HOOK A HUSBAND (AND A BABY)**
  by Carolyn Zane
  (YT#29, 10/96)

- **DISCOVERED: DADDY** by Marilyn Pappano
  (IM#746, 11/96)

Daddy Knows Last arrives in July...only from

DKL

Silhouette's recipe for a sizzling summer:

* Take the best-looking cowboy in South Dakota
* Mix in a brilliant bachelor
* Add a sexy, mysterious sheikh
* Combine their stories into one collection and you've got one sensational super-hot read!

Summer Sizzlers

MEN OF Summer

Three short stories by these favorite authors:

Kathleen Eagle
Joan Hohl
Barbara Faith

Available this July wherever Silhouette books are sold.

Look us up on-line at: http://www.romance.net

Silhouette®

SS9

What do women really want to know?

Trust the world's largest publisher of
women's fiction to tell you.

HARLEQUIN ULTIMATE GUIDES™

I CAN FIX THAT

A Guide For Women
Who Want To Do It Themselves

This is the only guide a self-reliant
woman will ever need to deal
with those pesky items that
break, wear out or just don't work
anymore. Chock-full of friendly
advice and straightforward,
step-by-step solutions to the
trials of everyday life in our
gadget-oriented world! So, don't
just sit there wondering how to
fix the VCR—run to your
nearest bookstore for your copy now!

Available this May, at your favorite retail outlet.

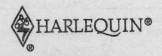

HARLEQUIN®

FI